Great Short Works

of

Henry van Dyke

Great Short Works
of
Henry van Dyke

Introduction
by ELLA DE MERS

A Perennial Classic
Harper & Row, Publishers
New York

Contents

Introduction by Ella De Mers vii

A Writer's Request of His Master 1

Preface to The Story of the Other Wise Man . . 3

The Story of the Other Wise Man 9

The Mansion 35

The Blue Flower 61

The Source 67

The Mill 83

A Handful of Clay 103

A Brave Heart 109

A Friend of Justice 129

The White Blot 149

The Keeper of the Light 171

Little Rivers 195

Introduction

In his essay "At the Sign of the Balsam Bough," Henry van Dyke wrote, "Among the mountains there is a gorge. And in the gorge there is a river. And in the river there is a pool. And in the pool there is an island. And on the island, for four happy days, there was a camp."

The Reverend Dr. van Dyke, pastor of the Brick Presbyterian Church of New York City, and his wife, along with their four French-Canadian guides, had found an almost inaccessible, altogether beautiful spot in the forest back of Lake St. John in Canada. As time benevolently slackened her pace, husband and wife relived their joy in earlier camping expeditions, excursions into nature that were central to their happiness and, for Henry van Dyke, to his very philosophy of life. It was early September, yet they had discovered a flower of June in bloom, its persistent message symbolic to the poet-husband of a renewal of the dreams of their youth.

" 'And need we ever grow old?' asked my lady Greygown, as she sat that evening with the twin-flower on her breast, watching the stars come out along the edge of the cliffs, and tremble on the hurrying tide of the river. 'Must we grow old as well as grey? Is the time coming when all life will be commonplace and practical, and governed by a dull 'of course'? Shall we not always find adventures and romances, and a few blossoms returning, even when the season grows late?'

" 'At least,' I answered, 'let us believe in the possibility, for to doubt it is to destroy it. If we can only come back to nature together every year, and consider the flowers and the birds, and confess our faults and mistakes and our unbelief under these silent stars, and hear the river murmuring our absolution, we shall die young, even though we live long: we shall have a treasure of memories which will be like the twin-flower, always a double blossom on a single stem, and carry with us into the unseen world something which will make it worth while to be immortal.' "

Something which will make it worth while to be immortal. Although Henry van Dyke's dates straddle the turn of the century (1852-1933), they are weighted, as this suggestive exchange reveals, toward that core of idealism and transcendental thought which had characterized the earlier half of the nineteenth century. Romanticist by educational absorption, forthright moralist by religious heritage, he was a strenuously purposeful man, uniformly successful and prolific in many fields— as minister to both the Congregational and Presbyterian churches, as university professor, international statesman, poet, essayist, critic, anthologist, storyteller, lecturer, after-dinner speaker, and certainly not least, as a dedicated fisherman. Today, he is remembered, for the most part, as the author of "The Other Wise Man," that remarkable Christmas story which has slipped imperceptibly into the heart of a much older tradition all over the world. Here, as in all of his amazingly productive careers, his is the authoritative voice of the man with a message.

"I respond to what you say," he wrote in an 1898 letter, "about the possibility of literature and morality living together. An author is not a preacher, but I can't see why he should let the preacher monopolize all the best subjects. There are no themes in the world so real or so interesting as moral conflicts and problems. There are only two ways to handle them. The moral and the immoral way. I fail to see that the latter is any more artistic per se than the former." For this generation of modern readers, taught disillusion and detachment by the holocaust of two world wars, trained to look for at least two sides to every human problem in the literature of a highly relativistic society, confused by the ambiguities of good and evil in a world of pluralistic values, and finally and perhaps most significantly, alienated from nature by an impersonal science, it has been almost a relief to dismiss the moral response as outright over-simplification in the search for truth. Yet, the careful reader of Victorian literature is impressed not so much with the complexity of the revolution that in the nine-teenth century attacked long-established values in eco-nomics, in religion, and irrevocably in literature, but rather with the paradoxical simplicity of the religious reply.

A man should consume his own smoke, Henry van Dyke felt about his own doubts, his own moments of despair—this in keeping with the spare Calvinistic code he had inherited from his Dutch ancestors. Misgivings were to be recognized for what they were, moods, not to be accepted but to be assiduously resisted. "Life," the young junior at Princeton was to declare in his Chapel Stage oration, "is not a river bearing all along. It is rather a vast ocean with shifting streams and varying currents, shoals and reefs, in which only a boat with a rudder and a guiding principle can safely navigate." The rudder was his thorough religious inheritance, and in his formative years he had willingly embraced the principle. He had a Teacher who had defined the Way with a relentless clarity almost two thousand years ago:

Enter ye in at the strait gate: for wide is the gate and broad the way that leadeth to destruction, and many there be which go in thereat: Because strait is the gate and narrow is the way which leadeth unto life, and few there be that find it.

Young Henry had come by his religious faith honestly. Behind his father, a Presbyterian minister of consider-able stature in Brooklyn, New York, were seven genera-tions of transplanted Dutch Calvinists, strong in their faith, active for their church, the record claims, and, predictably, lovers of the out-of-doors. The relationship between father and son was unusually sensitive and strong. An ardent fisherman since his own Pennsylvania boyhood, the elder van Dyke had early initiated his son into that select company of anglers for whom fishing is not so much a hobby or a sport as it is a philosophy of life. Both father and son, and later the fortunate grandchildren, could claim their passionate love of land and water as a life-giving source of their faith and serenity. Again and again, in his sermons, his poems, and in his stories, Henry van Dyke uses the river as one of his most productive symbols, "a mark of deep significance," he was to write, "in the picture-language of man."

The Brooklyn in which the boy grew up in the fifties was, for all practical purposes, still a Dutch village at the threshold of its phenomenal growth. Although the streets were troughs of mud in the rain, there were bluebirds in the trees, old book shops on Nassau Street, oysters to eat at Fulton Market, and there was always the indulgent father who could be inveigled into a fishing excursion on the clear waters on Coney Island Creek and Sheepshead Bay. These were the days of Civil War, turbulent enough for the stiff-necked pastor who would not compromise his conservative principles with Abolitionist excess, but only too realistically bloody for the young son who had to defend in the streets both his father's independent thinking and their common integrity with his fists. An insatiable reader, Henry was educated in his father's library until he was ten, taught in more formal circumstances by colleagues of his father in neighboring private schools, and sent to the Brooklyn Collegiate and Polytechnic Institute at fifteen to prepare for college.

Entering the College of New Jersey at Princeton in 1869, he was to become one of her most illustrious and devoted alumni, destined to return thirty-one years later as the distinguished Murray Professor of English Literature. Nevertheless, at the close of his undergraduate and graduate years, years characterized by a successful and an often brilliant scholarship and terminating with a degree from the Princeton Theological Seminary, the young graduate of 1877 found himself torn between a desire to pursue a literary career and a compelling sense of dedication to the church. Poet and moralist had not yet fused into the mature man—the man to be fulfilled by the unifying ideal of service—and Henry found himself unaccountably adrift in those very currents of life which he had so stoutly rejected in his Chapel oration five years before. A wise father read his son clearly and sent the young man off for a year of study in Germany. There at the University of Berlin, where the ghosts of Goethe and Schiller still walked, Henry drank deeply of the *Kulturkampf*—and studied theology. When he returned home, refreshed and fortified with a handsome brown beard and a dashing suit of brown velvet in his suitcase, he was in serene command of his own ship. In 1879 he accepted the call to the United Congregational Church in Newport, Rhode Island, where he discovered and developed for three years his genius for inspired preaching, fortified in action with a vigorous pastoral service. From Newport he went with his young bride, the former Ellen Reid of Baltimore, to his exceptionally successful ministry at the Brick Presbyterian Church in New York City which, in the course of seventeen strenuous years, was to earn for him a national reputation.

The return, in 1900, to an academic life at Princeton was in part the answer to a writer's need for more time for his books and for his pen. Continuing to serve the pulpit whenever the need arose, Professor van Dyke found in his teaching and in his writing the same cohesive purpose he had applied to all the activity of his busy life. At Princeton he was to know well that other Presbyterian idealist, Woodrow Wilson, earlier as professor of jurisprudence and political economy, and later as university president. When Wilson's political drive carried him to the presidency of the United States, he appointed his former colleague to serve as minister to the Netherlands and Luxembourg, a critical post in those war-torn years. In 1917 in order to speak out freely for American involvement in the European war, he resigned his post and gave inexhaustibly of his many-sided talents to the war effort, joining, after the guns had ceased, in the furious and foredoomed battle for the establishment of the League of Nations. In 1923 he retired from Princeton where, at the close of the war, he had taught for four more happy, vital years. A distinguished, out-spoken, international personality, he had left ten years in which to find more "adventures and romances" and to lay up the last of the treasure of memories in preaching, writing, lecturing, traveling, and necessarily, of course, in fishing. Twin-flowered still, Lady Greygown and he were to celebrate a joyous golden anniversary at Avalon, his Princeton home, in 1931.

Achievement, the passage of time, and a final date. Yet, as anthologist and Tennysonian critic van Dyke himself has said of the English poet-laureate, the study of whose life and works had occupied much of his enthusiastic scholarship, it is in the work of a man that we find his biography. The key to Henry van Dyke's accomplishment lies, surely, in the ambivalent character of his creative imagination. For him, art and morality were complementary, and since he had resolved their conflicting claims upon literature within a deeply religious context, it was inevitable that he should come to believe, as his son and biographer, Tertius van Dyke, has pointed out, that to be a man was to hold all one's powers in the balanced service of a great ideal. In his vigorous crusading years the young preacher had recognized that to be out of fashion was to be uncomfortable:

It is hard to be earnest in a frivolous society. It is hard to be decent, spiritually-minded, and full of charity in a mercenary age. . . . There is such a thing as a moral atmosphere, and when it is saturated with the invisible germs of an epidemic it is not easy to be well and strong. Even those who do not take the disease are affected by its presence. The whole tone of their health is lowered and they must take care to make an effort or they will break down.

With all of his several talents Dr. van Dyke took care; yet as he himself would have recognized, it is just this vigilance, this carefully nurtured structuring of moral principle that has separated him from at least three generations of readers—if, indeed, as Halford Luccock has said,

1890 can be used as a convenient dividing line separating an age of confidence in nearly every realm from a succeeding one of skepticism and disillusion.

At first glance no one seems further removed from the dilemma of the modern reader than Henry van Dyke; more closely and rather selectively, however, no one speaks more directly to a generation foundering in a static state of emotional malaise and tortured by a too-public self-examination in literature than does the allegorist. Van Dyke's use of the older, classical story forms of allegory and parable was fortunate. The conventionalized symbolism surmounts the problems caused by a century's change in idiom, permitting new kinds of readers to supply new meanings to the old affirmations. In fact, Henry van Dyke has already moved into that rich half world of literature shared in the past by Swift and Defoe and in the present by Orwell and Golding, in which stories intended for adults have been pre-empted by children. The message reaches forth now in both directions, simply and directly to the child, more subtly and in ever-widening circles of meaning to the mature reader, depending, in allegory, on the vitality and the reach of his moral vision.

All the problems of a fractured society are here—alienation, detachment, and despair—in the stories from *The Blue Flower,* in "The Story of the Other Wise Man," in "The Mansion." Tigranes, the uncommitted, insists that the wisdom which knows its own ignorance is the greatest wisdom. He finds excuse for his own fear of involvement in his wise man's tolerance of the principle of evil as well as of the principle of the good. The darkness, he reminds his fellow Magi, is equal to the light, and the conflict between them will never be ended. In energetic opposition to the nostalgic Magian is John Weightman of "The Mansion" who willingly embraces the promise of the present but who does all the right things for the wrong reasons, the greatest of disservices in the ageless effort to put moral theory into practice. Finally, there is the pertinent timeliness of the choice of metaphor in "The Source." When the reservoirs of a great city dry up, the joyless residents worship the windlass, for how else can they bring water into their fields? Since they have a well-established system of inspection for the cisterns and the wells, carried out daily at every hour by the Princes of the Water, it does not occur to them to return to the source of their supply. Prophetic moralist and conservationist, Henry van Dyke was pleading for the preservation of the Adirondack region of forests and waters "in its pristine beauty" in a letter to the New York *Herald Tribune* as early as 1883!

For the general reader, his "outdoor essays" are among his best works, especially *Little Rivers,* published in 1895. "After many years," wrote Maxwell Struthers Burt in 1920 "I have read again *Little Rivers,* and again I received the same shock of delight, for here is sunlight and green shadows and warm open places made into words." A true son of the nineteenth century, absorbed and sustained by nature, Henry van Dyke follows in the path of the great Romanticists who had known a sublime, God-filled world. He is not a Wordsworth, seeking primarily the effect of nature on his own intense poetic imagination, nor yet is he an Emerson to whom every natural fact was inevitably a symbol of a spiritual fact, but rather he is the friendly fisherman who shares with his "gentle reader," in the true spirit of Izaak Walton, the sight, the sounds, the veritable goodness of the life-giving out-of-doors. All his nature essays, he says with a smile, "are nothing but a handful of variations on the old tune of 'Rest and be thankful,' a record of unconventional travel, a pilgrim's scrip with a few bits of blue-sky philosophy in it."

Surely a tune is burden light enough to carry into the unseen world—something to make it, perhaps, worthwhile to be immortal.

ELLA DE MERS

Trumbull, Connecticut
1965

A Writer's Request of His Master

Let me never tag a moral to a story, nor tell a story without a meaning. Make me respect my material so much that I dare not slight my work. Help me to deal very honestly with words and with people because they are both alive. Show me that as in a river, so in a writing, clearness is the best quality, and a little that is pure is worth more than much that is mixed. Teach me to see the local colour without being blind to the inner light. Give me an ideal that will stand the strain of weaving into human stuff on the loom of the real. Keep me from caring more for books than for folks, for art than for life. Steady me to do my full stint of work as well as I can: and when that is done, stop me, pay what wages Thou wilt, and help me to say,
from a quiet heart,
a grateful
AMEN.

Preface
to
The Story of
the Other Wise Man

It is now some years since this little story was set afloat on the sea of books. It is not a man-of-war, nor even a high-sided merchantman; only a small, peaceful sailing-vessel. Yet it has had rather an adventurous voyage. Twice it has fallen into the hands of pirates. The tides have carried it to far countries. It has been passed through the translator's port of entry into German, French, Armenian, Turkish, and perhaps some other foreign regions. Once I caught sight of it flying the outlandish flag of a brand-new phonetic language along the coasts of France; and once it was claimed by a dealer in antiquities as a long-lost legend of the Orient. Best of all, it has slipped quietly into many a far-away harbor that I have never seen, and found a kindly welcome, and brought back messages of good cheer from unknown friends.

Now it has turned home to be new-rigged and fitted for further voyaging. Before it is sent out again I have been asked to tell where the story came from and what it means.

I do not know where it came from—out of the air, perhaps. One thing is certain, it is not written in any other book, nor is it to be found among the ancient lore of the East. And yet I have never felt as if it were my own. It was a gift. It was sent to me; and it seemed as if I knew the Giver, though His name was not spoken.

The year had been full of sickness and sorrow. Every day brought trouble. Every night was tormented with pain. They are very long—those nights when one lies

3

awake, and hears the laboring heart pumping wearily at its task, and watches for the morning, not knowing whether it will ever dawn. They are not nights of fear; for the thought of death grows strangely familiar when you have lived with it for a year. Besides, after a time you come to feel like a soldier who has been long standing still under fire; any change would be a relief. But they are lonely nights; they are very heavy nights. And their heaviest burden is this:

You must face the thought that your work in the world may be almost ended, but you know that it is not nearly finished.

You have not solved the problems that perplexed you. You have not reached the goal that you aimed at. You have not accomplished the great task that you set for yourself. You are still on the way; and perhaps your journey must end now—nowhere—in the dark.

Well, it was in one of these long, lonely nights that this story came to me. I had studied and loved the curious tales of the Three Wise Men of the East as they are told in the *Golden Legend* of Jacobus de Voragine and other mediæval books. But of the Fourth Wise Man I had never heard until that night. Then I saw him distinctly, moving through the shadows in a little circle of light. His countenance was as clear as the memory of my father's face as I saw it for the last time a few months before. The narrative of his journeyings and trials and disappointments ran without a break. Even certain sentences came to me complete and unforgettable, clear-cut like a cameo. All that I had to do was to follow Artaban, step by step, as the tale went on, from the beginning to the end of his pilgrimage.

Perhaps this may explain some things in the story. I have been asked many times why I made the Fourth Wise Man tell a lie, in the cottage at Bethlehem, to save the little child's life.

I did not make him tell a lie.

What Artaban said to the soldiers he said for himself, because he could not help it.

Is a lie ever justifiable? Perhaps not. But may it not sometimes seem inevitable?

And if it were a sin, might not a man confess it, and be pardoned for it more easily than for the greater sin of spiritual selfishness, or indifference, or the betrayal of innocent blood? That is what I saw Artaban do. That is what I heard him say. All through his life he was trying to do the best that he could. It was not perfect. But there are some kinds of failure that are better than success.

Though the story of the Fourth Wise Man came to me suddenly and without labor, there was a great deal of study and toil to be done before it could be written down. An idea arrives without effort; a form can only be wrought out by patient labor. If your story is worth telling, you ought to love it enough to be willing to work over it until it is true—true not only to the ideal, but true also to the real. The light is a gift; but the local color can only be seen by one who looks for it long and steadily. Artaban went with me while I toiled through a score of volumes of ancient history and travel. I saw his figure while I journeyed on the motionless sea of the desert and in the strange cities of the East.

And now that his story is told, what does it mean?

How can I tell? What does life mean? If the meaning could be put into a sentence there would be no need of telling the story.

HENRY VAN DYKE.

The Story of
the Other Wise Man

The Story of the Other Wise Man

You know the story of the Three Wise Men of the East, and how they travelled from far away to offer their gifts at the manger-cradle in Bethlehem. But have you ever heard the story of the Other Wise Man, who also saw the star in its rising, and set out to follow it, yet did not arrive with his brethren in the presence of the young child Jesus? Of the great desire of this fourth pilgrim, and how it was denied, yet accomplished in the denial; of his many wanderings and the probations of his soul; of the long way of his seeking and the strange way of his finding the One whom he sought—I would tell the tale as I have heard fragments of it in the Hall of Dreams, in the palace of the Heart of Man.

I
The Sign in the Sky

In the days when Augustus Cæsar was master of many kings and Herod reigned in Jerusalem, there lived in the city of Ecbatana, among the mountains of Persia, a certain man named Artaban. His house stood close to the outermost of the walls which encircled the royal treasury. From his roof he could look over the seven-fold battlements of black and white and crimson and blue and red and silver and gold, to the hill where the summer palace of the Parthian emperors glittered like a jewel in a crown.

Around the dwelling of Artaban spread a fair garden, a tangle of flowers and fruit-trees, watered by a score of streams descending from the slopes of Mount Orontes, and made musical by innumerable birds. But all colour was lost in the soft and odorous darkness of the late September night, and all sounds were hushed in the deep charm of its silence, save the plashing of the water, like a voice half-sobbing and half-laughing under the shadows. High above the trees a dim glow of light shone through the curtained arches of the upper chamber, where the master of the house was holding council with his friends.

He stood by the doorway to greet his guests—a tall, dark man of about forty years, with brilliant eyes set near together under his broad brow, and firm lines graven around his fine, thin lips; the brow of a dreamer and the mouth of a soldier, a man of sensitive feeling but inflexible will—one of those who, in whatever age they may live, are born for inward conflict and a life of quest.

His robe was of pure white wool, thrown over a tunic of silk; and a white, pointed cap, with long lapels at the sides, rested on his flowing black hair. It was the dress of the ancient priesthood of the Magi, called the fire-worshippers.

"Welcome!" he said, in his low, pleasant voice, as one after another entered the room—"welcome, Abdus; peace be with you, Rhodaspes and Tigranes, and with you my father, Abgarus. You are all welcome. This house grows bright with the joy of your presence."

There were nine of the men, differing widely in age, but alike in the richness of their dress of many-coloured silks, and in the massive golden collars around their necks, marking them as Parthian nobles, and in the winged circles of gold resting upon their breasts, the sign of the followers of Zoroaster.

They took their places around a small black altar at the end of the room, where a tiny flame was burning. Artaban, standing beside it, and waving a barsom of thin tamarisk branches above the fire, fed it with dry sticks of pine and fragrant oils. Then he began the ancient chant of the Yasna, and the voices of his companions joined in the hymn to Ahura-Mazda:

> *We worship the Spirit Divine,*
> *   all wisdom and goodness possessing,*

Surrounded by Holy Immortals,
*   the givers of bounty and blessing;*
We joy in the work of His hands,
*   His truth and His power confessing.*

We praise all the things that are pure,
*   for these are His only Creation;*
The thoughts that are true, and the words
*   and the deeds that have won approbation;*
These are supported by Him,
*   and for these we make adoration.*

Hear us, O Mazda! Thou livest
*   in truth and in heavenly gladness;*
Cleanse us from falsehood, and keep us
*   from evil and bondage to badness;*
Pour out the light and the joy of Thy life
*   on our darkness and sadness.*

Shine on our gardens and fields,
*   shine on our working and weaving;*
Shine on the whole race of man,
*   believing and unbelieving;*
Shine on us now through the night,
Shine on us now in Thy might,
The flame of our holy love
*   and the song of our worship receiving.*

The fire rose with the chant, throbbing as if the flame responded to the music, until it cast a bright illumination through the whole apartment, revealing its simplicity and splendour.

The floor was laid with tiles of dark blue veined with white; pilasters of twisted silver stood out against the blue walls; the clear-story of round-arched windows above them was hung with azure silk; the vaulted ceiling was a pavement of blue stones, like the body of heaven in its clearness, sown with silver stars. From the four corners of the roof hung four golden magic-wheels, called the tongues of the gods. At the eastern end, behind the altar, there were two dark-red pillars of porphyry; above them a lintel of the same stone, on which was carved the figure of a winged archer, with his arrow set to the string and his bow drawn.

The doorway between the pillars, which opened upon the terrace of the roof, was covered with a heavy curtain of the colour of a ripe pomegranate, embroidered with innumerable golden rays shooting upward from the floor. In effect the room was like a quiet, starry night, all azure and silver, flushed in the east with rosy promise of the dawn. It was, as the house of a man should be, an expression of the character and spirit of the master.

He turned to his friends when the song was ended, and invited them to be seated on the divan at the western end of the room.

"You have come to-night," said he, looking around the circle, "at my call, as the faithful scholars of Zoroaster, to renew your worship and rekindle your faith in the God of Purity, even as this fire has been rekindled on the altar. We worship not the fire, but Him of whom it is the chosen symbol, because it is the purest of all created things. It speaks to us of one who is Light and Truth. Is it not so, my father?"

"It is well said, my son," answered the venerable Abgarus. "The enlightened are never idolaters. They lift the veil of form and go in to the shrine of reality, and new light and truth are coming to them continually through the old symbols."

"Hear me, then, my father and my friends," said Artaban, "while I tell you of the new light and truth that have come to me through the most ancient of all signs. We have searched the secrets of Nature together, and studied the healing virtues of water and fire and the plants. We have read also the books of prophecy in which the future is dimly foretold in words that are hard to understand. But the highest of all learning is the knowledge of the stars. To trace their course is to untangle the threads of the mystery of life from the beginning to the end. If we could follow them perfectly, nothing would be hidden from us. But is not our knowledge of them still incomplete? Are there not many stars still beyond our horizon—lights that are known only to the dwellers in the far south-land, among the spice-trees of Punt and the gold mines of Ophir?"

There was a murmur of assent among the listeners.

"The stars," said Tigranes, "are the thoughts of the Eternal. They are numberless. But the thoughts of man can be counted, like the years of his life. The wisdom of the Magi is the greatest of all wisdoms on earth, because it knows its own ignorance. And that is the secret of power. We keep men always looking and waiting for a new sunrise. But we ourselves understand that the darkness is equal to the light, and that the conflict between them will never be ended."

"That does not satisfy me," answered Artaban, "for, if the waiting must be endless, if there could be no fulfilment of it, then it would not be wisdom to look and wait. We should become like those new teachers of the Greeks, who say that there is no truth, and that the only wise men are those who spend their lives in discovering and exposing the lies that have been believed in the world. But the new sunrise will certainly appear in the appointed time. Do not our own books tell us that this will come to pass, and that men will see the brightness of a great light?"

"That is true," said the voice of Abgarus; "every faithful disciple of Zoroaster knows the prophecy of the Avesta, and carries the word in his heart. 'In that day Sosiosh the Victorious shall arise out of the number of the prophets in the east country. Around him shall shine a mighty brightness, and he shall make life everlasting, incorruptible, and immortal, and the dead shall rise again.' "

"This is a dark saying," said Tigranes, "and it may be that we shall never understand it. It is better to consider the things that are near at hand, and to increase the influence of the Magi in their own country, rather than to look for one who may be a stranger, and to whom we must resign our power."

The others seemed to approve these words. There was a silent feeling of agreement manifest among them; their looks responded with that indefinable expression which always follows when a speaker has uttered the thought that has been slumbering in the hearts of his listeners. But Artaban turned to Abgarus with a glow on his face, and said:

"My father, I have kept this prophecy in the secret place of my soul. Religion without a great hope would be like an altar without a living fire. And now the flame has burned more brightly, and by the light of it I have read other words which also have come from the fountain of Truth, and speak yet more clearly of the rising of the Victorious One in his brightness."

He drew from the breast of his tunic two small rolls of fine parchment, with writing upon them, and unfolded them carefully upon his knee.

"In the years that are lost in the past, long before our fathers came into the land of Babylon, there were wise men in Chaldea, from whom the first of the Magi learned the secret of the heavens. And of these Balaam the son of Beor was one of the mightiest. Hear the words of his prophecy: 'There shall come a star out of Jacob, and a sceptre shall arise out of Israel.' "

The lips of Tigranes drew downward with contempt, as he said:

"Judah was a captive by the waters of Babylon, and the sons of Jacob were in bondage to our kings. The tribes of Israel are scattered through the mountains like lost sheep, and from the remnant that dwells in Judea under the yoke of Rome neither star nor sceptre shall arise."

"And yet," answered Artaban, "it was the Hebrew Daniel, the mighty searcher of dreams, the counsellor of kings, the wise Belteshazzar, who was most honoured and beloved of our great King Cyrus. A prophet of sure things and a reader of the thoughts of the Eternal, Daniel proved himself to our people. And these are the words that he wrote." (Artaban read from the second roll:) " 'Know, therefore, and understand that from the going forth of the commandment to restore Jerusalem, unto the Anointed One, the Prince, the time shall be seven and threescore and two weeks.' "

"But, my son," said Abgarus, doubtfully, "these are

mystical numbers. Who can interpret them, or who can find the key that shall unlock their meaning?"

Artaban answered: "It has been shown to me and to my three companions among the Magi—Caspar, Melchior, and Balthazar. We have searched the ancient tablets of Chaldea and computed the time. It falls in this year. We have studied the sky, and in the spring of the year we saw two of the greatest planets draw near together in the sign of the Fish, which is the house of the Hebrews. We also saw a new star there, which shone for one night and then vanished. Now again the two great planets are meeting. This night is their conjunction. My three brothers are watching by the ancient Temple of the Seven Spheres, at Borsippa, in Babylonia, and I am watching here. If the star shines again, they will wait ten days for me at the temple, and then we will set out together for Jerusalem, to see and worship the promised one who shall be born King of Israel. I believe the sign will come. I have made ready for the journey. I have sold my possessions, and bought these three jewels—a sapphire, a ruby, and a pearl—to carry them as tribute to the King. And I ask you to go with me on the pilgrimage, that we may have joy together in finding the Prince who is worthy to be served."

While he was speaking he thrust his hand into the inmost fold of his girdle and drew out three great gems—one blue as a fragment of the night sky, one redder than a ray of sunrise, and one as pure as the peak of a snow-mountain at twilight—and laid them on the outspread scrolls before him.

But his friends looked on with strange and alien eyes. A veil of doubt and mistrust came over their faces, like a fog creeping up from the marshes to hide the hills. They glanced at each other with looks of wonder and pity, as those who have listened to incredible sayings, the story of a wild vision, or the proposal of an impossible enterprise.

At last Tigranes said: "Artaban, this is a vain dream. It comes from too much looking upon the stars and the cherishing of lofty thoughts. It would be wiser to spend the time in gathering money for the new fire-temple at

Chala. No king will ever rise from the broken race of Israel, and no end will ever come to the eternal strife of light and darkness. He who looks for it is a chaser of shadows. Farewell."

And another said: "Artaban, I have no knowledge of these things, and my office as guardian of the royal treasure binds me here. The quest is not for me. But if thou must follow it, fare thee well."

And another said: "In my house there sleeps a new bride, and I cannot leave her nor take her with me on this strange journey. This quest is not for me. But may thy steps be prospered wherever thou goest. So, farewell."

And another said: "I am ill and unfit for hardship, but there is a man among my servants whom I will send with thee when thou goest, to bring me word how thou farest."

So, one by one, they left the house of Artaban. But Abgarus, the oldest and the one who loved him the best, lingered after the others had gone, and said, gravely: "My son, it may be that the light of truth is in this sign that has appeared in the skies, and then it will surely lead to the Prince and the mighty brightness. Or it may be that it is only a shadow of the light, as Tigranes has said, and then he who follows it will have a long pilgrimage and a fruitless search. But it is better to follow even the shadow of the best than to remain content with the worst. And those who would see wonderful things must often be ready to travel alone. I am too old for this journey, but my heart shall be a companion of thy pilgrimage day and night, and I shall know the end of thy quest. Go in peace."

Then Abgarus went out of the azure chamber with its silver stars, and Artaban was left in solitude.

He gathered up the jewels and replaced them in his girdle. For a long time he stood and watched the flame that flickered and sank upon the altar. Then he crossed the hall, lifted the heavy curtain, and passed out between the pillars of porphyry to the terrace on the roof.

The shiver that runs through the earth ere she rouses from her night-sleep had already begun, and the cool wind that heralds the daybreak was drawing downward from the lofty snow-traced ravines of Mount Orontes. Birds, half-awakened, crept and chirped among the rustling leaves, and the smell of ripened grapes came in brief wafts from the arbours.

Far over the eastern plain a white mist stretched like a lake. But where the distant peaks of Zagros serrated the western horizon the sky was clear. Jupiter and Saturn rolled together like drops of lambent flame about to blend in one.

As Artaban watched them, a steel-blue spark was born out of the darkness beneath, rounding itself with purple splendours to a crimson sphere, and spiring upward through rays of saffron and orange into a point of white radiance. Tiny and infinitely remote, yet perfect in every part, it pulsated in the enormous vault as if the three jewels in the Magian's girdle had mingled and been transformed into a living heart of light.

He bowed his head. He covered his brow with his hands. "It is the sign," he said. "The King is coming, and I will go to meet him."

II
By the Waters of Babylon

All night long, Vasda, the swiftest of Artaban's horses, had been waiting, saddled and bridled, in her stall, pawing the ground impatiently, and shaking her bit as if she shared the eagerness of her master's purpose, though she knew not its meaning.

Before the birds had fully roused to their strong, high, joyful chant of morning song, before the white mist had begun to lift lazily from the plain, the Other Wise Man was in the saddle, riding swiftly along the high-road, which skirted the base of Mount Orontes, westward.

How close, how intimate is the comradeship between a man and his favourite horse on a long journey. It is a silent, comprehensive friendship, an intercourse beyond the need of words.

They drink at the same way-side springs, and sleep under the same guardian stars. They are conscious together of the subduing spell of nightfall and the quickening joy of daybreak. The master shares his evening meal with his hungry companion, and feels the soft, moist lips caressing the palm of his hand as they close over the morsel of bread. In the gray dawn he is roused from his bivouac by the gentle stir of a warm, sweet breath over his sleeping face, and looks up into the eyes of his faithful fellow-traveller, ready and waiting for the toil of the day. Surely, unless he is a pagan and an unbeliever, by whatever name he calls upon his God, he will thank Him for this voiceless sympathy, this dumb affection, and his morning prayer will embrace a double blessing—God bless us both, the horse and the rider, and keep our feet from falling and our souls from death!

Then, through the keen morning air, the swift hoofs beat their tattoo along the road, keeping time to the pulsing of two hearts that are moved with the same eager desire—to conquer space, to devour the distance, to attain the goal of the journey.

Artaban must indeed ride wisely and well if he would keep the appointed hour with the other Magi; for the route was a hundred and fifty parasangs, and fifteen was the utmost that he could travel in a day. But he knew Vasda's strength, and pushed forward without anxiety, making the fixed distance every day, though he must travel late into the night, and in the morning long before sunrise.

He passed along the brown slopes of Mount Orontes, furrowed by the rocky courses of a hundred torrents.

He crossed the level plains of the Nisæans, where the famous herds of horses, feeding in the wide pastures, tossed their heads at Vasda's approach, and galloped away with a thunder of many hoofs, and flocks of wild birds rose suddenly from the swampy meadows, wheeling in great circles with a shining flutter of innumerable wings and shrill cries of surprise.

He traversed the fertile fields of Concabar, where the dust from the threshing-floors filled the air with a golden mist, half hiding the huge temple of Astarte with its four hundred pillars.

At Baghistan, among the rich gardens watered by fountains from the rock, he looked up at the mountain thrusting its immense rugged brow out over the road, and saw the figure of King Darius trampling upon his fallen foes, and the proud list of his wars and conquests graven high upon the face of the eternal cliff.

Over many a cold and desolate pass, crawling painfully across the wind-swept shoulders of the hills; down many a black mountain-gorge, where the river roared and raced before him like a savage guide; across many a smiling vale, with terraces of yellow limestone full of vines and fruit-trees; through the oak-groves of Carine and the dark Gates of Zagros, walled in by precipices; into the ancient city of Chala, where the people of Samaria had been kept in captivity long ago; and out again by the mighty portal, riven through the encircling hills, where he saw the image of the High Priest of the Magi sculptured on the wall of rock, with hand uplifted as if to bless the centuries of pilgrims; past the entrance of the narrow defile, filled from end to end with orchards of peaches and figs, through which the river Gyndes foamed down to meet him; over the broad rice-fields, where the autumnal vapours spread their deathly mists; following along the course of the river, under tremulous shadows of poplar and tamarind, among the lower hills; and out upon the flat plain, where the road ran straight as an arrow through the stubble-fields and parched meadows; past the city of Ctesiphon, where the Parthian emperors reigned, and the vast metropolis of Seleucia which Alexander built; across the swirling floods of Tigris and the many channels of Euphrates, flowing yellow through the corn-lands—Artaban pressed onward until he arrived, at nightfall on the tenth day, beneath the shattered walls of populous Babylon.

Vasda was almost spent, and Artaban would gladly have turned into the city to find rest and refreshment for himself and for her. But he knew that it was three hours' journey yet to the Temple of the Seven Spheres, and he must reach the place by midnight if he would find his comrades waiting. So he did not halt, but rode steadily across the stubble-fields.

A grove of date-palms made an island of gloom in the pale yellow sea. As she passed into the shadow Vasda slackened her pace, and began to pick her way more carefully.

Near the farther end of the darkness an access of caution seemed to fall upon her. She scented some danger or difficulty; it was not in her heart to fly from it—only to be prepared for it, and to meet it wisely, as a good horse should do. The grove was close and silent as the tomb; not a leaf rustled, not a bird sang.

She felt her steps before her delicately, carrying her head low, and sighing now and then with apprehension. At last she gave a quick breath of anxiety and dismay, and stood stock-still, quivering in every muscle, before a dark object in the shadow of the last palm-tree.

Artaban dismounted. The dim starlight revealed the form of a man lying across the road. His humble dress and the outline of his haggard face showed that he was probably one of the Hebrews who still dwelt in great numbers around the city. His pallid skin, dry and yellow as parchment, bore the mark of the deadly fever which ravaged the marsh-lands in autumn. The chill of death was in his lean hand, and, as Artaban released it, the arm fell back inertly upon the motionless breast.

He turned away with a thought of pity, leaving the body to that strange burial which the Magians deemed most fitting—the funeral of the desert, from which the kites and vultures rise on dark wings, and the beasts of prey slink furtively away. When they are gone there is only a heap of white bones on the sand.

But, as he turned, a long, faint, ghostly sigh came from the man's lips. The bony fingers gripped the hem of the Magian's robe and held him fast.

Artaban's heart leaped to his throat, not with fear, but with a dumb resentment at the importunity of this blind delay.

How could he stay here in the darkness to minister to a

dying stranger? What claim had this unknown fragment of human life upon his compassion or his service? If he lingered but for an hour he could hardly reach Borsippa at the appointed time. His companions would think he had given up the journey. They would go without him. He would lose his quest.

But if he went on now, the man would surely die. If Artaban stayed, life might be restored. His spirit throbbed and fluttered with the urgency of the crisis. Should he risk the great reward of his faith for the sake of a single deed of charity? Should he turn aside, if only for a moment, from the following of the star, to give a cup of cold water to a poor, perishing Hebrew?

"God of truth and purity," he prayed, "direct me in the holy path, the way of wisdom which Thou only knowest."

Then he turned back to the sick man. Loosening the grasp of his hand, he carried him to a little mound at the foot of the palm-tree.

He unbound the thick folds of the turban and opened the garment above the sunken breast. He brought water from one of the small canals near by, and moistened the sufferer's brow and mouth. He mingled a draught of one of those simple but potent remedies which he carried always in his girdle—for the Magians were physicians as well as astrologers—and poured it slowly between the colourless lips. Hour after hour he laboured as only a skilful healer of disease can do. At last the man's strength returned; he sat up and looked about him.

"Who art thou?" he said, in the rude dialect of the country, "and why hast thou sought me here to bring back my life?"

"I am Artaban the Magian, of the city of Ecbatana, and I am going to Jerusalem in search of one who is to be born King of the Jews, a great Prince and Deliverer of all men. I dare not delay any longer upon my journey, for the caravan that has waited for me may depart without me. But see, here is all that I have left of bread and wine, and here is a potion of healing herbs. When thy strength is restored thou canst find the dwellings of the Hebrews among the houses of Babylon."

The Jew raised his trembling hand solemnly to heaven.

"Now may the God of Abraham and Isaac and Jacob bless and prosper the journey of the merciful, and bring him in peace to his desired haven. Stay! I have nothing to give thee in return—only this: that I can tell thee where the Messiah must be sought. For our prophets have said that he should be born not in Jerusalem, but in Bethlehem of Judah. May the Lord bring thee in safety to that place, because thou hast had pity upon the sick."

It was already long past midnight. Artaban rode in haste, and Vasda, restored by the brief rest, ran eagerly through the silent plain and swam the channels of the river. She put forth the remnant of her strength, and fled over the ground like a gazelle.

But the first beam of the rising sun sent a long shadow before her as she entered upon the final stadium of the journey, and the eyes of Artaban, anxiously scanning the great mound of Nimrod and the Temple of the Seven Spheres, could discern no trace of his friends.

The many-coloured terraces of black and orange and red and yellow and green and blue and white, shattered by the convulsions of nature, and crumbling under the repeated blows of human violence, still glittered like a ruined rainbow in the morning light.

Artaban rode swiftly around the hill. He dismounted and climbed to the highest terrace, looking out toward the west.

The huge desolation of the marshes stretched away to the horizon and the border of the desert. Bitterns stood by the stagnant pools and jackals skulked through the low bushes; but there was no sign of the caravan of the Wise Men, far or near.

At the edge of the terrace he saw a little cairn of broken bricks, and under them a piece of papyrus. He caught it up and read: "We have waited past the midnight, and can delay no longer. We go to find the King. Follow us across the desert."

Artaban sat down upon the ground and covered his head in despair.

"How can I cross the desert," said he, "with no food

and with a spent horse? I must return to Babylon, sell my sapphire, and buy a train of camels, and provision for the journey. I may never overtake my friends. Only God the merciful knows whether I shall not lose the sight of the King because I tarried to show mercy."

III
For the Sake of a Little Child

There was a silence in the Hall of Dreams, where I was listening to the story of the Other Wise Man. Through this silence I saw, but very dimly, his figure passing over the dreary undulations of the desert, high upon the back of his camel, rocking steadily onward like a ship over the waves.

The land of death spread its cruel net around him. The stony waste bore no fruit but briers and thorns. The dark ledges of rock thrust themselves above the surface here and there, like the bones of perished monsters. Arid and inhospitable mountain-ranges rose before him, furrowed with dry channels of ancient torrents, white and ghastly as scars on the face of nature. Shifting hills of treacherous sand were heaped like tombs along the horizon. By day, the fierce heat pressed its intolerable burden on the quivering air. No living creature moved on the dumb, swooning earth, but tiny jerboas scuttling through the parched bushes, or lizards vanishing in the clefts of the rock. By night the jackals prowled and barked in the distance, and the lion made the black ravines echo with his hollow roaring, while a bitter, blighting chill followed the fever of the day. Through heat and cold, the Magian moved steadily onward.

Then I saw the gardens and orchards of Damascus, watered by the streams of Abana and Pharpar, with their sloping swards inlaid with bloom, and their thickets of myrrh and roses. I saw the long, snowy ridge of Hermon, and the dark groves of cedars, and the valley of the Jordan, and the blue waters of the Lake of Galilee, and the fertile plain of Esdraelon, and the hills of Ephraim, and the highlands of Judah. Through all these I followed the figure of Artaban moving steadily onward, until he arrived at Bethlehem. And it was the third day after the three Wise Men had come to that place and had found Mary and Joseph, with the young child, Jesus, and had laid their gifts of gold and frankincense and myrrh at his feet.

Then the Other Wise Man drew near, weary, but full of hope, bearing his ruby and his pearl to offer to the King. "For now at last," he said, "I shall surely find him, though I be alone, and later than my brethren. This is the place of which the Hebrew exile told me that the prophets had spoken, and here I shall behold the rising of the great light. But I must inquire about the visit of my brethren, and to what house the star directed them, and to whom they presented their tribute."

The streets of the village seemed to be deserted, and Artaban wondered whether the men had all gone up to the hill-pastures to bring down their sheep. From the open door of a cottage he heard the sound of a woman's voice singing softly. He entered and found a young mother hushing her baby to rest. She told him of the strangers from the far East who had appeared in the village three days ago, and how they said that a star had guided them to the place where Joseph of Nazareth was lodging with his wife and her new-born child, and how they had paid reverence to the child and given him many rich gifts.

"But the travellers disappeared again," she continued, "as suddenly as they had come. We were afraid at the strangeness of their visit. We could not understand it. The man of Nazareth took the child and his mother, and fled away that same night secretly, and it was whispered that they were going to Egypt. Ever since, there has been a spell upon the village; something evil hangs over it. They say that the Roman soldiers are coming from Jerusalem to force a new tax from us, and the men have driven the flocks and herds far back among the hills, and hidden themselves to escape it."

Artaban listened to her gentle, timid speech, and the

child in her arms looked up in his face and smiled, stretching out its rosy hands to grasp at the winged circle of gold on his breast. His heart warmed to the touch. It seemed like a greeting of love and trust to one who had journeyed long in loneliness and perplexity, fighting with his own doubts and fears, and following a light that was veiled in clouds.

"Why might not this child have been the promised Prince?" he asked within himself, as he touched its soft cheek. "Kings have been born ere now in lowlier houses than this, and the favourite of the stars may rise even from a cottage. But it has not seemed good to the God of wisdom to reward my search so soon and so easily. The one whom I seek has gone before me; and now I must follow the King to Egypt."

The young mother laid the baby in its cradle, and rose to minister to the wants of the strange guest that fate had brought into her house. She set food before him, the plain fare of peasants, but willingly offered, and therefore full of refreshment for the soul as well as for the body. Artaban accepted it gratefully; and, as he ate, the child fell into a happy slumber, and murmured sweetly in its dreams, and a great peace filled the room.

But suddenly there came the noise of a wild confusion in the streets of the village, a shrieking and wailing of women's voices, a clangour of brazen trumpets and a clashing of swords, and a desperate cry: "The soldiers! the soldiers of Herod! They are killing our children."

The young mother's face grew white with terror. She clasped her child to her bosom, and crouched motionless in the darkest corner of the room, covering him with the folds of her robe, lest he should wake and cry.

But Artaban went quickly and stood in the doorway of the house. His broad shoulders filled the portal from side to side, and the peak of his white cap all but touched the lintel.

The soldiers came hurrying down the street with bloody hands and dripping swords. At the sight of the stranger in his imposing dress they hesitated with surprise. The captain of the band approached the threshold to thrust him aside. But Artaban did not stir. His face was as calm as though he were watching the stars, and in his eyes there burned that steady radiance before which even the half-tamed hunting leopard shrinks, and the blood-hound pauses in his leap. He held the soldier silently for an instant, and then said in a low voice:

"I am all alone in this place, and I am waiting to give this jewel to the prudent captain who will leave me in peace."

He showed the ruby, glistening in the hollow of his hand like a great drop of blood.

The captain was amazed at the splendour of the gem. The pupils of his eyes expanded with desire, and the hard lines of greed wrinkled around his lips. He stretched out his hand and took the ruby.

"March on!" he cried to his men, "there is no child here. The house is empty."

The clamour and the clang of arms passed down the street as the headlong fury of the chase sweeps by the secret covert where the trembling deer is hidden. Artaban re-entered the cottage. He turned his face to the east and prayed:

"God of truth, forgive my sin! I have said the thing that is not, to save the life of a child. And two of my gifts are gone. I have spent for man that which was meant for God. Shall I ever be worthy to see the face of the King?"

But the voice of the woman, weeping for joy in the shadow behind him, said very gently:

"Because thou has saved the life of my little one, may the Lord bless thee and keep thee; the Lord make His face to shine upon thee and be gracious unto thee; the Lord lift up His countenance upon thee and give thee peace."

IV

In the Hidden Way of Sorrow

Again there was a silence in the Hall of Dreams, deeper and more mysterious than the first interval, and I understood that the years of Artaban were flowing very swiftly under the stillness, and I caught only a glimpse, here and there, of the river of his life shining through the mist that concealed its course.

I saw him moving among the throngs of men in populous Egypt, seeking everywhere for traces of the household that had come down from Bethlehem, and finding them under the spreading sycamore-trees of Heliopolis, and beneath the walls of the Roman fortress of New Babylon beside the Nile—traces so faint and dim that they vanished before him continually, as footprints on the wet river-sand glisten for a moment with moisture and then disappear.

I saw him again at the foot of the pyramids, which lifted their sharp points into the intense saffron glow of the sunset sky, changeless monuments of the perishable glory and the imperishable hope of man. He looked up into the face of the crouching Sphinx and vainly tried to read the meaning of the calm eyes and smiling mouth. Was it, indeed, the mockery of all effort and all aspiration, as Tigranes had said—the cruel jest of a riddle that has no answer, a search that never can succeed? Or was there a touch of pity and encouragement in that inscrutable smile—a promise that even the defeated should attain a victory, and the disappointed should discover a prize, and the ignorant should be made wise, and the blind should see, and the wandering should come into the haven at last?

I saw him again in an obscure house of Alexandria, taking counsel with a Hebrew rabbi. The venerable man, bending over the rolls of parchment on which the prophecies of Israel were written, read aloud the pathetic words which foretold the sufferings of the promised Messiah—the despised and rejected of men, the man of sorrows and acquainted with grief.

"And remember, my son," said he, fixing his eyes upon the face of Artaban, "the King whom thou seekest is not to be found in a palace, nor among the rich and powerful. If the light of the world and the glory of Israel had been appointed to come with the greatness of earthly splendour, it must have appeared long ago. For no son of Abraham will ever again rival the power which Joseph had in the palaces of Egypt, or the magnificence of Solomon throned between the lions in Jerusalem. But the light for which the world is waiting is a new light, the glory that shall rise out of patient and triumphant suffering. And the kingdom which is to be established forever is a new kingdom, the royalty of unconquerable love.

"I do not know how this shall come to pass, nor how the turbulent kings and peoples of earth shall be brought to acknowledge the Messiah and pay homage to him. But this I know. Those who seek him will do well to look among the poor and the lowly, the sorrowful and the oppressed."

So I saw the Other Wise Man again and again, travelling from place to place, and searching among the people of the dispersion, with whom the little family from Bethlehem might, perhaps, have found a refuge. He passed through countries where famine lay heavy upon the land, and the poor were crying for bread. He made his dwelling in plague-stricken cities where the sick were languishing in the bitter companionship of helpless misery. He visited the oppressed and the afflicted in the gloom of subterranean prisons, and the crowded wretchedness of slave-markets, and the weary toil of galley-ships. In all this populous and intricate world of anguish, though he found none to worship, he found many to help. He fed the hungry, and clothed the naked, and healed the sick, and comforted the captive; and his years passed more swiftly than the weaver's shuttle that flashes back and forth through the loom while the web grows and the pattern is completed.

It seemed almost as if he had forgotten his quest. But once I saw him for a moment as he stood alone at sunrise, waiting at the gate of a Roman prison. He had taken from a secret resting-place in his bosom the pearl, the last of his jewels. As he looked at it, a mellower lustre, a soft and iridescent light, full of shifting gleams of azure and rose, trembled upon its surface. It seemed to have absorbed some reflection of the lost sapphire and ruby. So the secret purpose of a noble life draws into itself the memories of past joy and past sorrow. All that has helped it, all that has hindered it, is transfused by a subtle magic into its very essence. It becomes more luminous and precious the longer it is carried close to the warmth of the beating heart.

Then, at last, while I was thinking of this pearl, and of its meaning, I heard the end of the story of the Other Wise Man.

V
A Pearl of Great Price

Three-and-thirty years of the life of Artaban had passed away, and he was still a pilgrim and a seeker after light. His hair, once darker than the cliffs of Zagros, was now white as the wintry snow that covered them. His eyes, that once flashed like flames of fire, were dull as embers smouldering among the ashes.

Worn and weary and ready to die, but still looking for the King, he had come for the last time to Jerusalem. He had often visited the holy city before, and had searched all its lanes and crowded hovels and black prisons without finding any trace of the family of Nazarenes who had fled from Bethlehem long ago. But now it seemed as if he must make one more effort, and something whispered in his heart that, at last, he might succeed.

It was the season of the Passover. The city was thronged with strangers. The children of Israel, scattered in far lands, had returned to the Temple for the great feast, and there had been a confusion of tongues in the narrow streets for many days.

But on this day a singular agitation was visible in the multitude. The sky was veiled with a portentous gloom. Currents of excitement seemed to flash through the crowd. A secret tide was sweeping them all one way. The clatter of sandals and the soft, thick sound of thousands of bare feet shuffling over the stones, flowed unceasingly along the street that leads to the Damascus gate.

Artaban joined a group of people from his own country, Parthian Jews who had come up to keep the Passover, and inquired of them the cause of the tumult, and where they were going.

"We are going," they answered, "to the place called Golgotha, outside the city walls, where there is to be an execution. Have you not heard what has happened? Two famous robbers are to be crucified, and with them another, called Jesus of Nazareth, a man who has done many wonderful works among the people, so that they love him greatly. But the priests and elders have said that he must die, because he gave himself out to be the Son of God. And Pilate has sent him to the cross because he said that he was the 'King of the Jews.' "

How strangely these familiar words fell upon the tired heart of Artaban! They had led him for a lifetime over land and sea. And now they came to him mysteriously, like a message of despair. The King had arisen, but he had been denied and cast out. He was about to perish. Perhaps he was already dying. Could it be the same who had been born in Bethlehem thirty-three years ago, at whose birth the star had appeared in heaven, and of whose coming the prophets had spoken?

Artaban's heart beat unsteadily with that troubled, doubtful apprehension which is the excitement of old age. But he said within himself: "The ways of God are stranger than the thoughts of men, and it may be that I shall find the King, at last, in the hands of his enemies, and shall come in time to offer my pearl for his ransom before he dies."

So the old man followed the multitude with slow and painful steps toward the Damascus gate of the city. Just beyond the entrance of the guardhouse a troop of Macedonian soldiers came down the street, dragging a young girl with torn dress and dishevelled hair. As the Magian paused to look at her with compassion, she broke suddenly from the hands of her tormentors, and threw herself at his feet, clasping him around the knees. She had seen his white cap and the winged circle on his breast.

"Have pity on me," she cried, "and save me, for the sake of the God of Purity! I also am a daughter of the true religion which is taught by the Magi. My father was a merchant of Parthia, but he is dead, and I am seized for his debts to be sold as a slave. Save me from worse than death!"

Artaban trembled.

It was the old conflict in his soul, which had come to him in the palm-grove of Babylon and in the cottage at Bethlehem—the conflict between the expectation of faith and the impulse of love. Twice the gift which he had consecrated to the worship of religion had been drawn to the service of humanity. This was the third trial, the ultimate probation, the final and irrevocable choice.

Was it his great opportunity, or his last temptation? He could not tell. One thing only was clear in the darkness of his mind—it was inevitable. And does not the inevitable come from God?

One thing only was sure to his divided heart—to rescue this helpless girl would be a true deed of love. And is not love the light of the soul?

He took the pearl from his bosom. Never had it seemed so luminous, so radiant, so full of tender, living lustre. He laid it in the hand of the slave.

"This is thy ransom, daughter! It is the last of my treasures which I kept for the King."

While he spoke, the darkness of the sky deepened, and shuddering tremors ran through the earth heaving convulsively like the breast of one who struggles with mighty grief.

The walls of the houses rocked to and fro. Stones were loosened and crashed into the street. Dust clouds filled the air. The soldiers fled in terror, reeling like drunken men. But Artaban and the girl whom he had ransomed crouched helpless beneath the wall of the Prætorium.

What had he to fear? What had he to hope? He had given away the last remnant of his tribute for the King. He had parted with the last hope of finding him. The quest was over, and it had failed. But, even in that thought, accepted and embraced, there was peace. It was not resignation. It was not submission. It was something more profound and searching. He knew that all was well, because he had done the best that he could from day to day. He had been true to the light that had been given to him. He had looked for more. And if he had not found it, if a failure was all that came out of his life, doubtless that was the best that was possible. He had not seen the revelation of "life everlasting, incorruptible and immortal." But he knew that even if he could live his earthly life over again, it would not be otherwise than it had been.

One more lingering pulsation of the earthquake quivered through the ground. A heavy tile, shaken from the roof, fell and struck the old man on the temple. He lay breathless and pale, with his gray head resting on the young girl's shoulder, and the blood trickling from the wound. As she bent over him, fearing that he was dead, there came a voice through the twilight, very small and still, like music sounding from a distance, in which the notes are clear but the words are lost. The girl turned to see if some one had spoken from the window above them, but she saw no one.

Then the old man's lips began to move, as if in answer, and she heard him say in the Parthian tongue:

"Not so, my Lord! For when saw I thee an hungered and fed thee? Or thirsty, and gave thee drink? When saw I thee a stranger, and took thee in? Or naked, and clothed thee? When saw I thee sick or in prison, and came unto thee? Three-and-thirty years have I looked for thee; but I have never seen thy face, nor ministered to thee, my King."

He ceased, and the sweet voice came again. And again the maid heard it, very faint and far away. But now it seemed as though she understood the words:

"Verily I say unto thee, Inasmuch as thou has done it unto one of the least of these my brethren, thou hast done it unto me."

A calm radiance of wonder and joy lighted the pale face of Artaban like the first ray of dawn on a snowy mountain-peak. A long breath of relief exhaled gently from his lips.

His journey was ended. His treasures were accepted. The Other Wise Man had found the King.

The Mansion

The Mansion

There was an air of calm and reserved opulence about the Weightman mansion that spoke not of money squandered, but of wealth prudently applied. Standing on a corner of the Avenue no longer fashionable for residence, it looked upon the swelling tide of business with an expression of complacency and half-disdain.

The house was not beautiful. There was nothing in its straight front of chocolate-colored stone, its heavy cornices, its broad, staring windows of plate glass, its carved and bronze-bedecked mahogany doors at the top of the wide stoop, to charm the eye or fascinate the imagination. But it was eminently respectable, and in its way imposing. It seemed to say that the glittering shops of the jewelers, the milliners, the confectioners, the florists, the picture-dealers, the furriers, the makers of rare and costly antiquities, retail traders in luxuries of life, were beneath the notice of a house that had its foundations in the high finance, and was built literally and figuratively in the shadow of St. Petronius' Church.

At the same time there was something self-pleased and congratulatory in the way in which the mansion held its own amid the changing neighborhood. It almost seemed to be lifted up a little, among the tall buildings near at hand, as if it felt the rising value of the land on which it stood.

John Weightman was like the house into which he had built himself thirty years ago, and in which his ideals and ambitions were incrusted. He was a self-made man. But in making himself he had chosen a highly esteemed pattern and worked according to the approved rules. There was nothing irregular, questionable, flamboyant about him. He was solid, correct, and justly successful.

His minor tastes, of course, had been carefully kept up to date. At the proper time, pictures by the Barbizon masters, old English plate and portraits, bronzes by Barye and marbles by Rodin, Persian carpets and Chinese porcelains, had been introduced to the mansion. It contained a Louis Quinze reception-room, an Empire drawing-room, a Jacobean dining-room and various apartments dimly reminiscent of the styles of furniture affected by deceased monarchs. That the hallways were too short for the historic perspective did not make much difference. American decorative art is *capable de tout*, it absorbs all periods. Of each period Mr. Weightman wished to have something of the best. He understood its value, present as a certificate, and prospective as an investment.

It was only in the architecture of his town house that he remained conservative, immovable, one might almost say Early-Victorian-Christian. His country house at Dulwich-on-the-Sound was a palace of the Italian Renaissance. But in town he adhered to an architecture which had moral associations, the Nineteenth-Century-Brownstone epoch. It was a symbol of his social position, his religious doctrine, and even, in a way, of his business creed.

"A man of fixed principles," he would say, "should express them in the looks of his house. New York changes its domestic architecture too rapidly. It is like divorce. It is not dignified. I don't like it. Extravagance and fickleness are advertised in most of these new houses. I wish to be known for different qualities. Dignity and prudence are the things that people trust. Every one knows that I can afford to live in the house that suits me. It is a guarantee to the public. It inspires confidence. It helps my influence. There is a text in the Bible about 'a house that hath foundations.' That is the proper kind of a mansion for a solid man."

Harold Weightman had often listened to his father discoursing in this fashion on the fundamental principles of life, and always with a divided mind. He admired immensely his father's talents and the single-minded energy with which he improved them. But in the paternal philosophy there was something that disquieted and oppressed the young man, and made him gasp inwardly for fresh air and free action.

At times, during his college course and his years at the law school, he had yielded to this impulse and broken away—now toward extravagance and dissipation, and then, when the reaction came, toward a romantic devotion to work among the poor. He had felt his father's disapproval for both of these forms of imprudence; but it was never expressed in a harsh or violent way, always with a certain tolerant patience, such as one might show for the mistakes and vagaries of the very young. John Weightman was not hasty, impulsive, inconsiderate, even toward his own children. With them, as with the rest of the world, he felt that he had a reputation to maintain, a theory to vindicate. He could afford to give them time to see that he was absolutely right.

One of his favorite Scripture quotations was, "Wait on the Lord." He had applied it to real estate and to people, with profitable results.

But to human persons the sensation of being waited for is not always agreeable. Sometimes, especially with the young, it produces a vague restlessness, a dumb resentment, which is increased by the fact that one can hardly explain or justify it. Of this John Weightman was not conscious. It lay beyond his horizon. He did not take it into account in the plan of life which he made for himself and for his family as the sharers and inheritors of his success.

"Father plays us," said Harold, in a moment of irritation, to his mother, "like pieces in a game of chess."

"My dear," said that lady, whose faith in her husband was religious, "you ought not to speak so impatiently. At least he wins the game. He is one of the most respected men in New York. And he is very generous, too."

"I wish he would be more generous in letting us be ourselves," said the young man. "He always has something in view for us and expects to move us up to it."

"But isn't it always for our benefit?" replied his mother. "Look what a position we have. No one cay say there is any taint on our money. There are no rumors about your father. He has kept the laws of God and of man. He has never made any mistakes."

Harold got up from his chair and poked the fire. Then he came back to the ample, well-gowned, firm-looking lady, and sat beside her on the sofa. He took her hand gently and looked at the two rings—a thin band of yellow gold, and a small solitaire diamond—which kept their place on her third finger in modest dignity, as if not shamed, but rather justified, by the splendor of the emerald which glittered beside them.

"Mother," he said, "you have a wonderful hand. And father made no mistake when he won you. But are you sure he has always been so inerrant?"

"Harold," she exclaimed, a little stiffly, "what do you mean? His life is an open book."

"Oh," he answered, "I don't mean anything bad, mother dear. I know the governor's life is an open book— a ledger, if you like, kept in the best bookkeeping hand, and always ready for inspection—every page correct, and showing a handsome balance. But isn't it a mistake not to allow us to make our own mistakes, to learn for ourselves, to live our own lives? Must we be always working for 'the balance,' in one thing or another? I want to be myself—to get outside of this everlasting, profitable 'plan' —to let myself go, and lose myself for a while at least—to do the things that I want to do, just because I want to do them."

"My boy," said his mother, anxiously, "you are not going to do anything wrong or foolish? You know the falsehood of that old proverb about wild oats."

He threw back his head and laughed. "Yes, mother," he answered, "I know it well enough. But in California, you know, the wild oats are one of the most valuable crops. They grow all over the hillsides and keep the cattle and the horses alive. But that wasn't what I meant— to sow wild oats. Say to pick wild flowers, if you like, or even to chase wild geese—to do something that seems good to me just for its own sake, not for the sake of wages of one kind or another. I feel like a hired man, in the serv-

ice of this magnificent mansion—say in training for
father's place as majordomo. I'd like to get out some way,
to feel free—perhaps to do something for others."

The young man's voice hesitated a little. "Yes, it
sounds like cant, I know, but sometimes I feel as if I'd
like to do some good in the world, if father only wouldn't
insist upon God's putting it into the ledger."

His mother moved uneasily, and a slight look of be-
wilderment came into her face.

"Isn't that almost irreverent?" she asked. "Surely the
righteous must have their reward. And your father is
good. See how much he gives to all the established charities, how many things he has founded. He's always thinking of others, and planning for them. And surely, for us,
he does everything. How well he has planned this trip to
Europe for me and the girls—the court-presentation at
Berlin, the season on the Riviera, the visits in England
with the Plumptons and the Halverstones. He says Lord
Halverstone has the finest old house in Sussex, pure Eliza-
bethan, and all the old customs are kept up, too—family
prayers every morning for all the domestics. By-the-way,
you know his son Bertie, I believe."

Harold smiled a little to himself as he answered: "Yes,
I fished at Catalina Island last June with the Honorable
Ethelbert; he's rather a decent chap, in spite of his in-
growing mind. But you?—mother, you are simply magnificent! You are father's masterpiece." The young man
leaned over to kiss her, and went up to the Riding Club
for his afternoon canter in the Park.

So it came to pass, early in December, that Mrs.
Weightman and her two daughters sailed for Europe, on
their serious pleasure trip, even as it had been written
in the book of Providence; and John Weightman, who
had made the entry, was left to pass the rest of the winter
with his son and heir in the brownstone mansion.

They were comfortable enough. The machinery of the
massive establishment ran as smoothly as a great electric dynamo. They were busy enough, too. John Weightman's plans and enterprises were complicated, though

his principle of action was always simple—to get good value for every expenditure and effort. The banking-house of which he was the chief, the brain, the will, the absolutely controlling hand, was so admirably organized that the details of its direction took but little time. But the scores of other interests that radiated from it and were dependent upon it—or perhaps it would be more accurate to say, that contributed to its solidity and success—the many investments, industrial, political, benevolent, reformatory, ecclesiastical, that had made the name of Weightman well known and potent in city, church, and state, demanded much attention and careful steering, in order that each might produce the desired result. There were board meetings of corporations and hospitals, conferences in Wall Street and at Albany, consultations and committee meetings in the brownstone mansion.

For a share in all this business and its adjuncts John Weightman had his son in training in one of the famous law firms of the city; for he held that banking itself is a simple affair, the only real difficulties of finance are on its legal side. Meantime he wished the young man to meet and know the men with whom he would have to deal when he became a partner in the house. So a couple of dinners were given in the mansion during December, after which the father called the son's attention to the fact that over a hundred million dollars had sat around the board.

But on Christmas Eve father and son were dining together without guests, and their talk across the broad table, glittering with silver and cut glass, and softly lit by shaded candles, was intimate, though a little slow at times. The elder man was in rather a rare mood, more expansive and confidential than usual; and, when the coffee was brought in and they were left alone, he talked more freely of his personal plans and hopes than he had ever done before.

"I feel very grateful to-night," said he, at last; "it must be something in the air of Christmas that gives me this feeling of thankfulness for the many divine mercies that have been bestowed upon me. All the principles by which I have tried to guide my life have been justified. I have never made the value of this salted almond by any-thing that the courts would not uphold, at least in the long run, and yet—or wouldn't it be truer to say and therefore?—my affairs have been wonderfully prospered. There's a great deal in that text 'Honesty is the best'—but no, that's not from the Bible, after all, is it? Wait a moment; there is something of that kind, I know."

"May I light a cigar, father," said Harold, turning away to hide a smile, "while you are remembering the text?"

"Yes, certainly," answered the elder man, rather shortly; "you know I don't dislike the smell. But it is a wasteful, useless habit, and therefore I have never prac-tised it. Nothing useless is worth while, that's my motto—nothing that does not bring the reward. Oh, now I recall the text, 'Verily I say unto you they have their reward.' I shall ask Doctor Snodgrass to preach a sermon on that verse some day."

"Using you as an illustration?"

"Well, not exactly that; but I could give him some good material from my own experience to prove the truth of Scripture. I can honestly say that there is not one of my charities that has not brought me in a good return, either in the increase of influence, the building up of credit, or the association with substantial people. Of course you have to be careful how you give, in order to secure the best results—no indiscriminate giving—no pennies in beg-gars' hats! It has been one of my principles always to use the same kind of judgment in charities that I use in my other affairs, and they have not disappointed me."

"Even the check that you put in the plate when you take the offertory up the aisle on Sunday morning?"

"Certainly; though there the influence is less direct; and I must confess that I have my doubts in regard to the collection for Foreign Missions. That always seems to me romantic and wasteful. You never hear from it in any definite way. They say the missionaries have done a good deal to open the way for trade; perhaps—but they have also gotten us into commercial and political difficul-ties. Yet I give to them—a little—it is a matter of conscience with me to identify myself with all the enterprises of the Church; it is the mainstay of social order and a prosperous civilization. But the best forms of benevolence are the well-established, organized ones here at home, where people can see them and know what they are doing."

"You mean the ones that have a local habitation and a name."

"Yes; they offer by far the safest return, though of course there is something gained by contributing to general funds. A public man can't afford to be without public spirit. But on the whole I prefer a building, or an endowment. There is a mutual advantage to a good name and a good institution in their connection in the public mind. It helps them both. Remember that, my boy. Of course at the beginning you will have to practise it in a small way; later, you will have larger opportunities. But try to put your gifts where they can be identified and do good all around. You'll see the wisdom of it in the long run."

"I can see it already, sir, and the way you describe it looks amazingly wise and prudent. In other words, we must cast our bread on the waters in large loaves, carried by sound ships marked with the owner's name, so that the return freight will be sure to come back to us."

The father laughed, but his eyes were frowning a little as if he suspected something irreverent under the respectful reply.

"You put it humourously, but there's sense in what you say. Why not? God rules the sea; but He expects us to follow the laws of navigation and commerce. Why not take good care of your bread, even when you give it away?"

"It's not for me to say why not—and yet I can think of cases—" The young man hesitated for a moment. His half-finished cigar had gone out. He rose and tossed it into the fire, in front of which he remained standing—a slender, eager, restless young figure, with a touch of hunger in the fine face, strangely like the unlike the father, at whom he looked with half-wistful curiosity.

"The fact is, sir," he continued, "there is such a case

in my mind now, and it is a good deal on my heart, too. So I thought of speaking to you about it to-night. You remember Tom Rollins, the Junior who was so good to me when I entered college?"

The father nodded. He remembered very well indeed the annoying incidents of his son's first escapade, and how Rollins had stood by him and helped to avoid a public disgrace, and how a close friendship had grown between the two boys, so different in their fortunes.

"Yes," he said, "I remember him. He was a promising young man. Has he succeeded?"

"Not exactly—that is, not yet. His business has been going rather badly. He has a wife and little baby, you know. And now he has broken down—something wrong with his lungs. The doctor says his only chance is a year or eighteen months in Colorado. I wish we could help him."

"How much would it cost?"

"Three or four thousand perhaps, as a loan."

"Does the doctor say he will get well?"

"A fighting chance—the doctor says."

The face of the older man changed subtly. Not a line was altered, but it seemed to have a different substance, as if it were carved out of some firm, imperishable stuff.

"A fighting chance," he said, "may do for a speculation, but it is not a good investment. You owe something to young Rollins. Your grateful feeling does you credit. But don't overwork it. Send him three or four hundred, if you like. You'll never hear from it again, except in the letter of thanks. But for Heaven's sake don't be sentimental. Religion is not a matter of sentiment; it's a matter of principle."

The face of the younger man changed now. But instead of becoming fixed and graven, it seemed to melt into life by the heat of an inward fire. His nostrils quivered with quick breath, his lips were curled.

"Principle!" he said. "You mean principal—and interest too. Well, sir, you know best whether that is religion or not. But if it is, count me out, please. Tom saved me from going to the devil, six years ago; and I'll be damned if I don't help him to the best of my ability now."

John Weightman looked at his son steadily. "Harold," he said at last, "you know I dislike violent language, and it never has any influence with me. If I could honestly approve of this proposition of yours, I'd let you have the money; but I can't; it's extravagant and useless. But you have your Christmas check for a thousand dollars coming to you to-morrow. You can use it as you please. I never interfere with your private affairs."

"Thank you," said Harold. "Thank you very much! But there's another private affair. I want to get away from this life, this town, this house. It stifles me. You refused last summer when I asked you to let me go up to Grenfell's Mission on the Labrador. I could go now, at least as far as the Newfoundland Station. Have you changed your mind?"

"Not at all. I think it is an exceedingly foolish enterprise. It would interrupt the career that I have marked out for you."

"Well, then, here's a cheaper proposition. Algy Vanderhoof wants me to join him on his yacht with—well, with a little party—to cruise in the West Indies. Would you prefer that?"

"Certainly not! The Vanderhoof set is wild and godless —I do not wish to see you keeping company with fools who walk in the broad and easy way that leads to perdition."

"It is rather a hard choice," said the young man, with a short laugh, turning toward the door. "According to you there's very little difference—a fool's paradise or a fool's hell! Well, it's one or the other for me, and I'll toss up for it to-night: heads, I lose; tails, the devil wins. Anyway, I'm sick of this, and I'm out of it."

"Harold," said the older man (and there was a slight tremor in his voice), "don't let us quarrel on Christmas Eve. All I want is to persuade you to think seriously of the duties and responsibilities to which God has called you —don't speak lightly of heaven and hell—remember, there is another life."

The young man came back and laid his hand upon his father's shoulder.

"Father," he said, "I want to remember it. I try to believe in it. But somehow or other, in this house, it all seems unreal to me. No doubt all you say is perfectly right and wise. I don't venture to argue against it, but I can't feel it—that's all. If I'm to have a soul, either to lose or to save, I must really live. Just now neither the present nor the future means anything to me. But surely we won't quarrel. I'm very grateful to you, and we'll part friends. Good-night, sir."

The father held out his hand in silence. The heavy portière dropped noiselessly behind the son, and he went up the wide, curving stairway to his own room.

Meantime John Weightman sat in his carved chair in the Jacobean dining-room. He felt strangely old and dull. The portraits of beautiful women by Lawrence and Reynolds and Raeburn, which had often seemed like real company to him, looked remote and uninteresting. He fancied something cold and almost unfriendly in their expression, as if they were staring through him or beyond him. They cared nothing for his principles, his hopes, his disappointments, his successes; they belonged to another world, in which he had no place. At this he felt a vague resentment, a sense of discomfort that he could not have defined or explained. He was used to being considered, respected, appreciated at his full value in every region, even in that of his own dreams.

Presently he rang for the butler, telling him to close the house and not to sit up, and walked with lagging steps into the long library, where the shaded lamps were burning. His eye fell upon the low shelves full of costly books, but he had no desire to open them. Even the carefully chosen pictures that hung above them seemed to have lost their attraction. He paused for a moment before an idyll of Corot—a dance of nymphs around some forgotten altar in a vaporous glade—and looked at it curiously. There was something rapturous and serene about the picture, a breath of spring-time in the misty trees, a harmony of joy in the dancing figures, that wakened in him a feeling of half-pleasure and half-envy. It represented something that he had never known in his calculated, orderly life. He was dimly mistrustful of it.

"It is certainly very beautiful," he thought, "but it is distinctly pagan; that altar is built to some heathen god. It does not fit into the scheme of a Christian life. I doubt whether it is consistent with the tone of my house. I will sell it this winter. It will bring three or four times what I paid for it. That was a good purchase, a very good bargain."

He dropped into the revolving chair before his big library table. It was covered with pamphlets and reports of the various enterprises in which he was interested. There was a pile of newspaper clippings in which his name was mentioned with praise for his sustaining power as a pillar of finance, for his judicious benevolence, for his support of wise and prudent reform movements, for his discretion in making permanent public gifts—"the Weightman Charities," one very complaisant editor called them, as if they deserved classification as a distinct species.

He turned the papers over listlessly. There was a description and a picture of the "Weightman Wing of the Hospital for Cripples," of which he was president; and an article on the new professor in the "Weightman Chair of Political Jurisprudence" in Jackson University, of which he was a trustee; and an illustrated account of the opening of the "Weightman Grammar-School" at Dulwich-on-the-Sound, where he had his legal residence for purposes of taxation.

This last was perhaps the most carefully planned of all the Weightman Charities. He desired to win the confidence and support of his rural neighbors. It had pleased him much when the local newspaper had spoken of him as an ideal citizen and the logical candidate for the Governorship of the State; but upon the whole it seemed to him wiser to keep out of active politics. It would be easier and better to put Harold into the running, to have him sent to the Legislature from the Dulwich district, then to the national House, then to the Senate. Why not? The Weightman interests were large enough to need a direct representative and guardian at Washington.

But to-night all these plans came back to him with dust upon them. They were dry and crumbling like forsaken habitations. The son upon whom his complacent ambition had rested had turned his back upon the mansion of his father's hopes. The break might not be final; and in any event there would be much to live for; the fortunes of the family would be secure. But the zest of it all would be gone if John Weightman had to give up the assurance of perpetuating his name and his principles in his son. It was a bitter disappointment, and he felt that he had not deserved it.

He rose from the chair and paced the room with leaden feet. For the first time in his life his age was visibly upon him. His head was heavy and hot, and the thoughts that rolled in it were confused and depressing. Could it be that he had made a mistake in the principles of his existence? There was no argument in what Harold had said—it was almost childish—and yet it had shaken the elder man more deeply than he cared to show. It held a silent attack which touched him more than open criticism.

Suppose the end of his life were nearer than he thought —the end must come some time—what if it were now? Had he not founded his house upon a rock? Had he not kept the Commandments? Was he not, "touching the law, blameless"? And beyond this, even if there were some faults in his character—and all men are sinners—yet he surely believed in the saving doctrines of religion— the forgiveness of sins, the resurrection of the body, the life everlasting. Yes, that was the true source of comfort, after all. He would read a bit in the Bible, as he did every night, and go to bed and to sleep.

He went back to his chair at the library table. A strange weight of weariness rested upon him, but he opened the book at a familiar place, and his eyes fell upon the verse at the bottom of the page.

"Lay not up for yourselves treasures upon earth."

That had been the text of the sermon a few weeks before. Sleepily, heavily, he tried to fix his mind upon it and recall it. What was it that Doctor Snodgrass had said? Ah, yes—that it was a mistake to pause here in reading the verse. We must read on without a pause—*Lay not up treasures upon earth where moth and rust do corrupt and where thieves break through and steal*—that was the true doctrine. We may have treasures upon earth, but they must not be put into unsafe places, but into safe places. A most comforting doctrine! He had always followed it. Moths and rust and thieves had done no harm to his investments.

John Weightman's drooping eyes turned to the next verse, at the top of the second column.

"But lay up for yourselves treasures in heaven."

Now what had the Doctor said about that? How was it to be understood—in what sense—treasures—in heaven?

The book seemed to float away from him. The light vanished. He wondered dimly if this could be Death, coming so suddenly, so quietly, so irresistibly. He struggled for a moment to hold himself up, and then sank slowly forward upon the table. His head rested upon his folded hands. He slipped into the unknown.

How long afterward conscious life returned to him he did not know. The blank might have been an hour or a century. He knew only that something had happened in the interval. What it was he could not tell. He found great difficulty in catching the thread of his identity again. He felt that he was himself; but the trouble was to make his connections, to verify and place himself, to know who and where he was.

At last it grew clear. John Weightman was sitting on a stone, not far from a road in a strange land.

The road was not a formal highway, fenced and graded. It was more like a great travel-trace, worn by thousands of feet passing across the open country in the same direction. Down in the valley, into which he could look, the road seemed to form itself gradually out of many minor paths; little footways coming across the meadows, winding tracks following along beside the streams, faintly marked trails emerging from the woodlands. But on the hillside the threads were more firmly woven into one clear band of travel, though there were still a few dim paths joining it here and there, as if persons had been climbing up the hill by other ways and had turned at last to seek the road.

From the edge of the hill, where John Weightman sat, he could see the travelers, in little groups or larger companies, gathering from time to time by the different paths, and making the ascent. They were all clothed in white, and the form of their garments was strange to him; it was like some old picture. They passed him, group after group, talking quietly together or singing; not moving in haste, but with a certain air of eagerness and joy as if they were glad to be on their way to an appointed place. They did not stay to speak to him, but they looked at him often and spoke to one another as they looked; and now and then one of them would smile and beckon him a friendly greeting, so that he felt they would like him to be with them.

There was quite an interval between the groups; and he followed each of them with his eyes after it had passed, blanching the long ribbon of the road for a little transient space, rising and receding across the wide, billowy upland, among the rounded hillocks of aerial green and gold and lilac, until it came to the high horizon, and stood outlined for a moment, a tiny cloud of whiteness against the tender blue, before it vanished over the hill.

For a long time he sat there watching and wondering. It was a very different world from that in which his mansion on the Avenue was built; and it looked strange to him, but most real—as real as anything he had ever seen. Presently he felt a strong desire to know what country it was and where the people were going. He had a faint premonition of what it must be, but he wished to be sure. So he rose from the stone where he was sitting, and came down through the short grass and the lavender flowers, toward a passing group of people. One of them turned to meet him, and held out his hand. It was an old man, under whose white beard and brows John Weightman thought he saw a suggestion of the face of the village doctor who had cared for him years ago, when he was a boy in the country.

"Welcome," said the old man. "Will you come with us?"

"Where are you going?"

"To the heavenly city, to see our mansions there."

"And who are these with you?"

"Strangers to me, until a little while ago; I know them better now. But you I have known for a long time, John Weightman. Don't you remember your old doctor?"

"Yes," he cried—"yes; your voice has not changed at all. I'm glad indeed to see you, Doctor McLean, especially now. All this seems very strange to me, almost oppressive. I wonder if—but may I go with you, do you suppose?"

"Surely," answered the doctor, with his familiar smile; "it will do you good. And you also must have a mansion in the city waiting for you—a fine one, too—are you not looking forward to it?"

"Yes," replied the other, hesitating a moment: "yes—I believe it must be so, although I had not expected to see it so soon. But I will go with you, and we can talk by the way."

The two men quickly caught up with the other people, and all went forward together along the road. The doctor had little to tell of his experience, for it had been a plain, hard life, uneventfully spent for others, and the story of the village was very simple. John Weightman's adventures and triumphs would have made a far richer, more imposing history, full of contacts with the great events and personages of the time. But somehow or other he did not care to speak much about it, walking on that wide heavenly moorland, under that tranquil, sunless arch of blue, in that free air of perfect peace, where the light was diffused without a shadow, as if the spirit of life in all things were luminous.

There was only one person besides the doctor in that little company whom John Weightman had known before —an old bookkeeper who had spent his life over a desk, carefully keeping accounts—a rusty, dull little man, patient and narrow, whose wife had been in the insane asylum for twenty years and whose only child was a crippled daughter, for whose comfort and happiness he had toiled and sacrificed himself without stint. It was a surprise to find him here, as care-free and joyful as the rest.

The lives of others in the company were revealed in brief glimpses as they talked together—a mother, early widowed, who had kept her little flock of children together and labored through hard and heavy years to bring them up in purity and knowledge—a Sister of Charity who had devoted herself to the nursing of poor folk who were being eaten to death by cancer—a schoolmaster whose heart and life had been poured into his quiet work of training boys for a clean and thoughtful manhood—a medical missionary who had given up a brilliant career in science to take the charge of a hospital in darkest Africa—a beautiful woman with silver hair who had resigned her dreams of love and marriage to care for an invalid father, and after his death had made her life a long, steady search for ways of doing kindnesses to others—a poet who had walked among the crowded tenements of the great city, bringing cheer and comfort not only by his songs, but by his wise and patient works of practical aid—a paralyzed woman who had lain for thirty years upon her bed, helpless but not hopeless, succeeding by a miracle of courage in her single aim, never to complain, but always to impart a bit of her joy and peace to every one who came near her. All these, and other persons like them, people of little consideration in the world, but now seemingly all full of great contentment and an inward gladness that made their steps light, were in the company that passed along the road, talking together of things past and things to come, and singing now and then with clear voices from which the veil of age and sorrow was lifted.

John Weightman joined in some of the songs—which were familiar to him from their use in the church—at first with a touch of hesitation, and then more confidently. For as they went on his sense of strangeness and fear at

his new experience diminished, and his thoughts began
to take on their habitual assurance and complacency.
Were not these people going to the Celestial City? And was
not he in his right place among them? He had always
looked forward to this journey. If they were sure, each
one, of finding a mansion there, could not he be far more
sure? His life had been more fruitful than theirs. He had
been a leader, a founder of new enterprises, a pillar of
Church and State, a prince of the House of Israel. Ten
talents had been given him, and he had made them twenty.
His reward would be proportionate. He was glad that
his companions were going to find fit dwellings prepared
for them; but he thought also with a certain pleasure of
the surprise that some of them would feel when they saw
his appointed mansion.

So they came to the summit of the moorland and
looked over into the world beyond. It was a vast, green
plain, softly rounded like a shallow vase, and circled with
hills of amethyst. A broad, shining river flowed through
it, and many silver threads of water were woven across
the green; and there were borders of tall trees on the
banks of the river, and orchards full of roses abloom
along the little streams, and in the midst of all stood the
city, white and wonderful and radiant.

When the travelers saw it they were filled with awe
and joy. They passed over the little streams and among
the orchards quickly and silently, as if they feared to
speak lest the city should vanish.

The wall of the city was very low, a child could see
over it, for it was made only of precious stones, which
are never large. The gate of the city was not like a gate
at all, for it was not barred with iron or wood, but only
a single pearl, softly gleaming, marked the place where
the wall ended and the entrance lay open.

A person stood there whose face was bright and grave,
and whose robe was like the flower of the lily, not a woven
fabric, but a living texture. "Come in," he said to the
company of travelers; "you are at your journey's end,
and your mansions are ready for you."

John Weightman hesitated, for he was troubled by a

doubt. Suppose that he was not really, like his companions, at his journey's end, but only transported for a little while out of the regular course of his life into this mysterious experience? Suppose that, after all, he had not really passed through the door of death, like these others, but only through the door of dreams, and was walking in a vision, a living man among the blessed dead. Would it be right for him to go with them into the heavenly city? Would it not be a deception, a desecration, a deep and unforgivable offense? The strange, confusing question had no reason in it, as he very well knew; for if he was dreaming, then it was all a dream; but if his companions were real, then he also was with them in reality, and if they had died then he must have died too. Yet he could not rid his mind of the sense that there was a difference between them and him, and it made him afraid to go on. But, as he paused and turned, the Keeper of the Gate looked straight and deep into his eyes, and beckoned to him. Then he knew that it was not only right but necessary that he should enter.

They passed from street to street among fair and spacious dwellings, set in amaranthine gardens, and adorned with an infinitely varied beauty of divine simplicity. The mansions differed in size, in shape, in charm: each one seemed to have its own personal look of loveliness; yet all were alike in fitness to their place, in harmony with one another, in the addition which each made to the singular and tranquil splendor of the city.

As the little company came, one by one, to the mansions which were prepared for them, and their Guide beckoned to the happy inhabitant to enter in and take possession, there was a soft murmur of joy, half wonder and half recognition; as if the new and immortal dwelling were crowned with the beauty of surprise, lovelier and nobler than all the dreams of it had been; and yet also as if it were touched with the beauty of the familiar, the remembered, the long-loved. One after another the travelers were led to their own mansions, and went in gladly; and from within, through the open doorways, came sweet voices of welcome, and low laughter, and song.

At last there was no one left with the Guide but the two old friends, Doctor McLean and John Weightman. They were standing in front of one of the largest and fairest of the houses, whose garden glowed softly with radiant flowers. The Guide laid his hand upon the doctor's shoulder.

"This is for you," he said. "Go in; there is no more pain here, no more death, nor sorrow, nor tears; for your old enemies are all conquered. But all the good that you have done for others, all the help that you have given, all the comfort that you have brought, all the strength and love that you have bestowed upon the suffering, are here; for we have built them all into this mansion for you."

The good man's face was lighted with a still joy. He clasped his old friend's hand closely, and whispered: "How wonderful it is! Go on, you will come to your mansion next, it is not far away, and we shall see each other again soon, very soon."

So he went through the garden, and into the music within. The Keeper of the Gate turned to John Weightman with level, quiet, searching eyes. Then he asked, gravely:

"Where do you wish me to lead you now?"

"To see my own mansion," answered the man, with half-concealed excitement. "Is there not one here for me? You may not let me enter it yet, perhaps, for I must confess to you that I am only—"

"I know," said the Keeper of the Gate—"I know it all. You are John Weightman."

"Yes," said the man, more firmly than he had spoken at first, for it gratified him that his name was known. "Yes, I am John Weightman, Senior Warden of St. Petronius' Church. I wish very much to see my mansion here, if only for a moment. I believe that you have one for me. Will you take me to it?"

The Keeper of the Gate drew a little book from the breast of his robe and turned over the pages.

"Certainly," he said, with a curious look at the man, "your name is here; and you shall see your mansion if you will follow me."

It seemed as if they must have walked miles and miles,

through the vast city, passing street after street of houses larger and smaller, of gardens richer and poorer, but all full of beauty and delight. They came into a kind of suburb, where there were many small cottages, with plots of flowers, very lowly, but bright and fragrant. Finally they reached an open field, bare and lonely-looking. There were two or three little bushes in it, without flowers, and the grass was sparse and thin. In the center of the field was a tiny hut, hardly big enough for a shepherd's shelter. It looked as if it had been built of discarded things, scraps and fragments of other buildings, put together with care and pains, by some one who had tried to make the most of cast-off material. There was something pitiful and shamefaced about the hut. It shrank and drooped and faded in its barren field, and seemed to cling only by sufferance to the edge of the splendid city.

"This," said the Keeper of the Gate, standing still and speaking with a low, distinct voice—"this is your mansion, John Weightman."

An almost intolerable shock of grieved wonder and indignation choked the man for a moment so that he could not say a word. Then he turned his face away from the poor little hut and began to remonstrate eagerly with his companion.

"Surely, sir," he stammered, "you must be in error about this. There is something wrong—some other John Weightman—a confusion of names—the book must be mistaken."

"There is no mistake," said the Keeper of the Gate, very calmly; "here is your name, the record of your title and your possessions in this place."

"But how **could** such a house be prepared for me," cried the man, with a resentful tremor in his voice—"for me, after my long and faithful service? Is this a suitable mansion for one so well known and devoted? Why is it so pitifully small and mean? Why have you not built it large and fair, like the others?"

"That is all the material you sent us."

"What!"

"We have used all the material that you sent us," repeated the Keeper of the Gate.

"Now I know that you are mistaken," cried the man, with growing earnestness, "for all my life long I have been doing things that must have supplied you with material. Have you not heard that I have built a schoolhouse; the wing of a hospital; two—yes, three—small churches, and the greater part of a large one, the spire of St. Petro—"

The Keeper of the Gate lifted his hand.

"Wait," he said; "we know all these things. They were not ill done. But they were all marked and used as foundation for the name and mansion of John Weightman in the world. Did you not plan them for that?"

"Yes," answered the man, confused and taken aback, "I confess that I thought often of them in that way. Perhaps my heart was set upon that too much. But there are other things—my endowment for the college—my steady and liberal contributions to all the established charities —my support of every respectable—"

"Wait," said the Keeper of the Gate again. "Were not all these carefully recorded on earth where they would add to your credit? They were not foolishly done. Verily, you have had your reward for them. Would you be paid twice?"

"No," cried the man, with deepening dismay, "I dare not claim that. I acknowledge that I considered my own interest too much. But surely not altogether. You have said that these things were not foolishly done. They accomplished some good in the world. Does not that count for something?"

"Yes," answered the Keeper of the Gate, "it counts in the world—where you counted it. But it does not belong to you here. We have saved and used everything that you sent us. This is the mansion prepared for you."

As he spoke, his look grew deeper and more searching, like a flame of fire. John Weightman could not endure it. It seemed to strip him naked and wither him. He sank to the ground under a crushing weight of shame, covering his eyes with his hands and cowering face downward upon the stones. Dimly through the trouble of his mind he felt their hardness and coldness.

"Tell me, then," he cried, brokenly, "since my life has been so little worth, how came I here at all?"

"Through the mercy of the King"—the answer was like the soft tolling of a bell.

"And how have I earned it?" he murmured.

"It is never earned; it is only given," came the clear, low reply.

"But how have I failed so wretchedly," he asked, "in all the purpose of my life? What could I have done better? What is it that counts here?"

"Only that which is truly given," answered the bell-like voice. Only that good which is done for the love of doing it. Only those plans in which the welfare of others is the master thought. Only those labors in which the sacrifice is greater than the reward. Only those gifts in which the giver forgets himself."

The man lay silent. A great weakness, an unspeakable despondency and humiliation were upon him. But the face of the Keeper of the Gate was infinitely tender as he bent over him.

"Think again, John Weightman. Has there been nothing like that in your life?"

"Nothing," he sighed. "If there ever were such things, it must have been long ago—they were all crowded out —I have forgotten them."

There was an ineffable smile on the face of the Keeper of the Gate, and his hand made the sign of the cross over the bowed head as he spoke gently:

"These are the things that the King never forgets; and because there were a few of them in your life, you have a little place here."

The sense of coldness and hardness under John Weightman's hands grew sharper and more distinct. The feeling of bodily weariness and lassitude weighed upon him, but there was a calm, almost a lightness, in his heart as he listened to the fading vibrations of the silvery bell-tones. The chimney clock on the mantel had just ended the last stroke of seven as he lifted his head from the table. Thin, pale strips of the city morning were falling into the room through the narrow partings of the heavy curtains.

What was it that had happened to him? Had he been ill? Had he died and come to life again? Or had he only slept, and had his soul gone visiting in dreams? He sat for some time, motionless, not lost, but finding himself in thought. Then he took a narrow book from the table drawer, wrote a check, and tore it out.

He went slowly up the stairs, knocked very softly at his son's door, and, hearing no answer, entered without noise. Harold was asleep, his bare arm thrown above his head, and his eager face relaxed in peace. His father looked at him a moment with strangely shining eyes, and then tiptoed quietly to the writing-desk, found a pencil and a sheet of paper, and wrote rapidly:

"My dear boy, here is what you asked me for; do what you like with it, and ask for more if you need it. If you are still thinking of that work with Grenfell, we'll talk it over to-day after church. I want to know your heart better; and if I have made mistakes—"

A slight noise made him turn his head. Harold was sitting up in bed with wide-open eyes.

"Father!" he cried, "is that you?"

"Yes, my son," answered John Weightman; "I've come back—I mean I've come up—no, I mean come in— well, here I am, and God give us a good Christmas together."

The Blue Flower

The Blue Flower

I have borrowed a symbol from the old German poet and philosopher, Novalis, *to stand instead of a name. The Blue Flower which he used in his romance of* Heinrich von Ofterdingen *to symbolize Poetry, the object of his young hero's quest, I have used here to signify happiness, the satisfaction of the heart.*

The parents were abed and sleeping. The clock on the wall ticked loudly and lazily, as if it had time to spare. Outside the rattling windows there was a restless, whispering wind. The room grew light, and dark, and wondrous light again, as the moon played hide-and-seek through the clouds. The boy, wide-awake and quiet in his bed, was thinking of the Stranger and his stories.

"It was not what he told me about the treasures," he said to himself, "that was not the thing which filled me with so strange a longing. I am not greedy for riches. But the Blue Flower is what I long for. I can think of nothing else. Never have I felt so before. It seems as if I had been dreaming until now—or as if I had just slept over into a new world.

"Who cared for flowers in the old world where I used to live? I never heard of anyone whose whole heart was set upon finding a flower. But now I cannot even tell all that I feel—sometimes as happy as if I were enchanted. But when the flower fades from me, when I cannot see it in my mind, then it is like being very thirsty and all alone. That is what the other people could not understand.

"Once upon a time, they say, the animals and the trees and the flowers used to talk to people. It seems to me, every minute, as if they were just going to begin again. When I look at them I can see what they want to

61

say. There must be a great many words that I do not know; if I knew more of them perhaps I could understand things better. I used to love to dance, but now I like better to think after the music."

Gradually the boy lost himself in sweet fancies, and suddenly he found himself again, in the charmed land of sleep. He wandered in far countries, rich and strange; he traversed wild waters with incredible swiftness; marvellous creatures appeared and vanished; he lived with all sorts of men, in battles, in whirling crowds, in lonely huts. He was cast into prison. He fell into dire distress and want. All experiences seemed to be sharpened to an edge. He felt them keenly, yet they did not harm him. He died and came alive again; he loved to the height of passion, and then was parted forever from his beloved. At last, toward morning, as the dawn was stealing near, his soul grew calm, and the pictures showed more clear and firm.

It seemed as if he were walking alone through the deep woods. Seldom the daylight shimmered through the green veil. Soon he came to a rocky gorge in the mountains. Under the mossy stones in the bed of the stream, he heard the water secretly tinkling downward, ever downward, as he climbed upward.

The forest grew thinner and lighter. He came to a fair meadow on the slope of the mountain. Beyond the meadow was a high cliff, and in the face of the cliff an opening like the entrance to a path. Dark was the way, but smooth, and he followed easily on till he came near to a vast cavern from which a flood of radiance streamed to meet him.

As he entered he beheld a mighty beam of light which sprang from the ground, shattering itself against the roof in countless sparks, falling and flowing all together into a great pool in the rock. Brighter was the light-beam than molten gold, but silent in its rise, and silent in its fall. The sacred stillness of a shrine, a never-broken hush of joy and wonder, filled the cavern. Cool was the dripping radiance that softly trickled down the walls, and the light that rippled from them was pale blue.

But the pool, as the boy drew near and watched it, quivered and glanced with the ever-changing colours of a liquid opal. He dipped his hands in it and wet his lips. It seemed as if a lively breeze passed through his heart.

He felt an irresistible desire to bathe in the pool. Slipping off his clothes he plunged in. It was as if he bathed in a cloud of sunset. A celestial rapture flowed through him. The waves of the stream were like a bevy of nymphs taking shape around him, clinging to him with tender breasts, as he floated onward, lost in delight, yet keenly sensitive to every impression. Swiftly the current bore him out of the pool, into a hollow in the cliff. Here a dimness of slumber shadowed his eyes, while he felt the pressure of the loveliest dreams.

When he awoke again, he was aware of a new fulness of light, purer and steadier than the first radiance. He found himself lying on the green turf, in the open air, beside a little fountain, which sparkled up and melted away in silver spray. Dark-blue were the rocks that rose at a little distance, veined with white as if strange words were written upon them. Dark-blue was the sky, and cloudless.

All passion had dissolved away from him; every sound was music; every breath was peace; the rocks were like sentinels protecting him; the sky was like a cup of blessing full of tranquil light.

But what charmed him most, and drew him with resistless power, was a tall, clear-blue flower, growing beside the spring, and almost touching him with its broad, glistening leaves. Round about were many other flowers, of all hues. Their odours mingled in a perfect chord of fragrance. He saw nothing but the Blue Flower.

Long and tenderly he gazed at it, with unspeakable love. At last he felt that he must go a little nearer to it, when suddenly it began to move and change. The leaves glistened more brightly, and drew themselves up closely around the swiftly growing stalk. The flower bent itself toward him, and the petals showed a blue, spreading necklace of sapphires, out of which the lovely face of a girl smiled softly into his eyes. His sweet astonishment grew with the wondrous transformation.

All at once he heard his mother's voice calling him, and awoke in his parents' room, already flooded with the gold of the morning sun.

From the German of Novalis.

The Source

The Source

I

In the middle of the land that is called by its inhabitants Koorma, and by strangers the Land of the Half-forgotten, I was toiling all day long through heavy sand and grass as hard as wire. Suddenly, toward evening, I came upon a place where a gate opened in the wall of mountains, and the plain ran in through the gate, making a little bay of level country among the hills.

Now this bay was not brown and hard and dry, like the mountains above me, neither was it covered with tawny billows of sand like the desert along the edge of which I had wearily coasted. But the surface of it was smooth and green; and as the winds of twilight breathed across it they were followed by soft waves of verdure, with silvery turnings of the under sides of many leaves, like ripples on a quiet harbour. There were fields of corn, filled with silken rustling, and vineyards with long rows of trimmed maple-trees standing each one like an emerald goblet wreathed with vines, and flower-gardens as bright as if the earth had been embroidered with threads of blue and scarlet and gold, and olive-orchards frosted over with delicate and fragrant blossoms. Red-roofed cottages were scattered everywhere through the sea of greenery, and in the centre, like a white ship surrounded by a flock of little boats, rested a small, fair, shining city.

I wondered greatly how this beauty had come into being on the border of the desert. Passing through the fields and gardens and orchards, I found that they were all encircled and lined with channels full of running water. I followed up one of the smaller channels until it came to a larger stream, and as I walked on beside it, still going upward, it guided me into the midst of the city, where I saw a sweet, merry river flowing through the main street, with abundance of water and a very pleasant sound.

There were houses and shops and lofty palaces and all that makes a city, but the life and joy of all, and the one thing that I remember best, was the river. For in the open square at the edge of the city there were marble pools where the children might bathe and play; at the corners of the streets and on the sides of the houses there were fountains for the drawing of water; at every crossing a stream was turned aside to run out to the vineyards; and the river was the mother of them all.

There were but few people in the streets, and none of the older folk from whom I might ask counsel or a lodging; so I stood and knocked at the door of a house. It was opened by an old man, who greeted me with kindness and bade me enter as his guest. After much courteous entertainment, and when supper was ended, his friendly manner and something of singular attractiveness in his countenance led me to tell him of my strange journeyings in the land of Koorma and in other lands where I had been seeking the Blue Flower, and to inquire of him the name and the story of his city and the cause of the river which made it glad.

"My son," he answered, "this is the city which was called Ablis, that is to say, Forsaken. For long ago men lived here, and the river made their fields fertile, and their dwellings were full of plenty and peace. But because of many evil things which have been half-forgotten, the river was turned aside, or else it was dried up at its source in the high place among the mountains, so that the water flowed down no more. The channels and the trenches and the marble pools and the basins beside the houses remained, but they were empty. So the gardens withered; the fields were barren; the city was desolate; and in the broken cisterns there was scanty water.

"Then there came one from a distant country who was very sorrowful to see the desolation. He told the people that it was vain to dig new cisterns and to keep the channels and trenches clean; for the water had come only from above. The Source must be found again and reopened. The river would not flow unless they traced it back to the spring, and visited it continually, and offered prayers and praises beside it without ceasing. Then the spring would rise to an outpouring, and the water would run down plentifully to make the gardens blossom and the city rejoice.

"So he went forth to open the fountain; but there were few that went with him, for he was a poor man of lowly aspect, and the path upward was steep and rough. But his companions saw that as he climbed among the rocks little streams of water gushed from the places where he trod, and pools began to gather in the dry river-bed. He went more swiftly than they could follow him, and at length he passed out of their sight. A little farther on they came to the rising of the river and there, beside the overflowing Source, they found their leader lying dead."

"That was a strange thing," I cried, "and very pitiful. Tell me how it came to pass, and what was the meaning of it."

"I cannot tell the whole of the meaning," replied the old man, after a little pause, "for it was many years ago. But this poor man had many enemies in the city, chiefly among the makers of cisterns, who hated him for his words. I believe that they went out after him secretly and slew him. But his followers came back to the city; and as they came the river began to run down very gently after them. They returned to the Source day by day, bringing others with them; for they said that their leader was really alive, though the form of his life had changed, and that he met them in that high place while they remembered him and prayed and sang songs of praise. More and more the people learned to go with them, and the path grew plainer and easier to find. The more the Source was revisited, the more abundant it became, and the more it filled the river. All the channels and the basins were supplied with water, and men made new channels which were also filled. Some of those who were diggers of trenches and hewers of cisterns said that it was their work which had wrought the change. But the wisest and best among the people knew that it all came from the Source, and they taught that if it should ever again be forgotten and left unvisited the river would fail again and desolation return. So every day, from the gardens and orchards and the streets of the city, men and women and children have gone up the mountain-path with singing, to rejoice beside the spring from which the river flows and to remember the one who opened it. We call it the River Carita. And the name of the city is no more Ablis, but Saloma, which is Peace. And the name of him who died to find the Source for us is so dear that we speak it only when we pray.

"But there are many things yet to learn about our city, and some that seem dark and cast a shadow on my thoughts. Therefore, my son, I bid you to be my guest, for there is a room in my house for the stranger; and to-morrow and on the following days you shall see how life goes with us, and read, if you can, the secret of the city."

That night I slept well, as one who has heard a pleasant tale, with the murmur of running water woven through my dreams; and the next day I went out early into the streets, for I was curious to see the manner of the visitation of the Source.

Already the people were coming forth and turning their steps upward in the mountain-path beside the river. Some of them went alone, swiftly and in silence; others were in groups of two or three, talking as they went; others were in larger companies, and they sang together very gladly and sweetly. But there were many people who remained working in their fields or in their houses, or stayed talking on the corners of the streets. Therefore I joined myself to one of the men who walked alone and asked him why all the people did not go to the spring, since the life of the city depended upon it, and whether, perhaps, the way was so long and so hard that none but the strongest could undertake it.

"Sir," said he, "I perceive that you are a stranger, for the way is both short and easy, so that the children are those who most delight in it; and if a man were in great haste he could go there and return in a little while. But of those who remain behind, some are the busy ones who must visit the fountain at another hour; and some are the careless ones who take life as it comes and never think where it comes from; and some are those who do not believe in the Source and will hear nothing about it."

"How can that be?" I said; "do they not drink of the water, and does it not make their fields green?"

"It is true," he said; "but these men have made wells close by the river, and they say that these wells fill themselves; and they have digged channels through their gardens, and they say that these channels would always have water in them even though the spring should cease to flow. Some of them say also that it is an unworthy thing to drink from a source that another has opened, and that every man ought to find a new spring for himself; so they spend the hour of the visitation, and many more, in searching among the mountains where there is no path."

While I wondered over this, we kept on in the way. There was already quite a throng of people all going in the same direction. And when we came to the Source, which flowed from an opening in a cliff, almost like a chamber hewn in the rock, and made a little garden of wild-flowers around it as it fell, I heard the music of many voices and the beautiful name of him who had given his life to find the forgotten spring.

Then we came down again, singly and in groups, following the river. It seemed already more bright and full and joyous. As we passed through the gardens I saw men turning aside to make new channels through fields which were not yet cultivated. And as we entered the city I saw the wheels of the mills that ground the corn whirling more swiftly, and the maidens coming with their pitchers to draw from the brimming basins at the street corners, and the children laughing because the marble pools were so full that they could swim in them. There was plenty of water everywhere.

For many weeks I stayed in the city of Saloma, going up the mountain-path in the morning, and returning to the day of work and the evening of play. I found friends among the people of the city, not only among those who walked together in the visitation of the Source, but also among those who remained behind, for many of them were kind and generous, faithful in their work, and very pleasant in their conversation.

Yet there was something lacking between me and them. I came not onto firm ground with them, for all their warmth of welcome and their pleasant ways. They were by nature of the race of those who dwell ever in one place; even in their thoughts they went not far abroad. But I have been ever a seeker, and the world seems to me made to wander in, rather than to abide in one corner of it and never see what the rest has in store. Now this was what the people of Saloma could not understand, and for this reason I seemed to them always a stranger, an alien, a guest. The fixed circle of their life was like an invisible wall, and with the best will in the world they knew not how to draw me within it. And I, for my part, while I understood well their wish to rest and be at peace, could not quite understand the way in which it found fulfilment, nor share the repose which seemed to them all-sufficient and lasting. In their gardens I saw ever the same flowers, and none perfect. At their feasts I tasted ever the same food, and none that made an end of hunger. In their talk I heard ever the same words, and none that went to the depth of thought. The very quietude and fixity of their being perplexed and estranged me. What to them was permanent, to me was transient. They were inhabitants: I was a visitor.

The one in all the city of Saloma with whom I was most at home was Ruamie, the little granddaughter of the old man with whom I lodged. To her, a girl of thirteen, fair-eyed and full of joy, the wonted round of life had not yet grown to be a matter of course. She was quick to feel and answer the newness of every day that dawned. When a strange bird flew down from the mountains into the gardens, it was she that saw it and wondered at it. It was she that walked with me most often in the path to the Source. She went out with me to the fields in the morning and almost every day found wild-flowers that were new to me. At sunset she drew me to happy games of youths and children, where her fancy was never tired of weaving new turns to the familiar pastimes. In the dusk she would sit beside me in an arbour of honeysuckle and question me about the flower that I was seeking,—for to her I had often spoken of my quest.

"Is it blue," she asked, "as blue as the speedwell that grows beside the brook?"

"Yes, it is as much bluer than the speedwell, as the river is deeper than the brook."

"And is it bright," she asked, "as bright as the drops of dew that shine in the moonlight?"

"Yes, it is as much brighter than the drops of dew as the sun is clearer than the moon."

"And is it sweet," she asked, "as sweet as the honeysuckle when the day is warm and still?"

"Yes, it is as much sweeter than the honeysuckle as the night is stiller and more sweet than the day."

"Tell me again," she asked, "when you saw it, and why do you seek it?"

"Once I saw it when I was a boy, no older than you. Our house looked out toward the hills, far away and at sunset softly blue against the eastern sky. It was the day that we laid my father to rest in the little burying-ground among the cedar-trees. There was his father's grave, and his father's father's grave, and there were the places for my mother and for my two brothers and for my sister and for me. I counted them all, when the others had gone back to the house. I paced up and down alone, measuring the ground; there was room enough for us all; and in the western corner where a young elm-tree was growing,—that would be my place, for I was the youngest. How tall would the elm-tree be then? I had never thought of it before. It seemed to make me sad and restless,—wishing for something, I knew not what,— longing to see the world and to taste happiness before I must sleep beneath the elm-tree. Then I looked off to the blue hills, shadowy and dreamlike, the boundary of the little world that I knew. And there, in a cleft between the highest peaks I saw a wondrous thing: for the place at which I was looking seemed to come nearer and nearer to me; I saw the trees, the rocks, the ferns, the white road winding before me; the enfolding hills unclosed like leaves, and in the heart of them I saw a Blue Flower, so bright, so beautiful that my eyes filled with tears as I looked. It was like a face that smiled at me and promised something. Then I heard a call, like the note of a trumpet very far away, calling me to come. And as I listened the flower faded into the dimness of the hills."

"Did you follow it," asked Ruamie, "and did you go away from your home? How could you do that?"

"Yes, Ruamie, when the time came, as soon as I was free, I set out on my journey, and my home is at the end of the journey, wherever that may be."

"And the flower," she asked, "you have seen it again?"

"Once again, when I was a youth, I saw it. After a long voyage upon stormy seas, we came into a quiet haven, and there the friend who was dearest to me, said good-by, for he was going back to his own country and his father's house, but I was still journeying onward. So as I stood at the bow of the ship, sailing out into the wide blue water, far away among the sparkling waves I saw a little island, with shores of silver sand and slopes of fairest green, and in the middle of the island the Blue Flower was growing, wondrous tall and dazzling, brighter than the sapphire of the sea. Then the call of the distant trumpet came floating across the water, and while it was sounding a shimmer of fog swept over the island and I could see it no more."

"Was it a real island," asked Ruamie. "Did you ever find it?"

"Never; for the ship sailed another way. But once again I saw the flower; three days before I came to Saloma. It was on the edge of the desert, close under the shadow of the great mountains. A vast loneliness was round about me; it seemed as if I was the only soul living upon earth; and I longed for the dwellings of men. Then as I woke in the morning I looked up at the dark ridge of the mountains, and there against the brightening blue of the sky I saw the Blue Flower standing up clear and brave. It shone so deep and pure that the sky grew pale around it. Then the echo of the far-off trumpet drifted down the hillsides, and the sun rose, and the flower was melted away in light. So I rose and travelled on till I came to Saloma."

"And now," said the child, "you are at home with us. Will you not stay for a long, long while? You may find the Blue Flower here. There are many kinds in the fields. I find new ones every day."

"I will stay while I can, Ruamie," I answered, taking her hand in mine as we walked back to the house at night-fall, "but how long that may be I cannot tell. For with you I am at home, yet the place where I must abide is the place where the flower grows, and when the call comes I must follow it."

"Yes," said she, looking at me half in doubt, "I think I understand. But wherever you go I hope you will find the flower at last."

In truth there were many things in the city that troubled me and made me restless, in spite of the sweet comfort of Ruamie's friendship and the tranquillity of the life in Saloma. I came to see the meaning of what the old man had said about the shadow that rested upon his thoughts. For there were some in the city who said that the hours of visitation were wasted, and that it would be better to employ the time in gathering water from the pools that formed among the mountains in the rainy season, or in sinking wells along the edge of the desert. Others had newly come to the city and were teaching that there was no Source, and that the story of the poor man who re-opened it was a fable, and that the hours of visitation were only hours of dreaming. There were many who believed them, and many more who said that it did not matter whether their words were true or false, and that it was of small moment whether men went to visit the fountain or not, provided only that they worked in the gardens and kept the marble pools and basins in repair and opened new canals through the fields, since there al-ways had been and always would be plenty of water.

As I listened to these sayings it seemed to me doubtful

what the end of the city would be. And while this doubt was yet heavy upon me, I heard at midnight the faint calling of the trumpet, sounding along the crest of the mountains: and as I went out to look where it came from, I saw, through the glimmering veil of the milky way, the shape of a blossom of celestial blue, whose petals seemed to fall and fade as I looked. So I bade farewell to the old man in whose house I had learned to love the hour of visitation and the Source and the name of him who opened it; and I kissed the hands and the brow of the little Ruamie who had entered my heart, and went forth sadly from the land of Koorma into other lands, to look for the Blue Flower.

II

In the Book of the Voyage without a Harbour is written the record of the ten years which passed before I came back again to the city of Saloma.

It was not easy to find, for I came down through the mountains, and as I looked from a distant shoulder of the hills for the little bay full of greenery, it was not to be seen. There was only a white town shining far off against the brown cliffs, like a flake of mica in a cleft of the rocks. Then I slept that night, full of care, on the hillside, and rising before dawn, came down in the early morning toward the city.

The fields were lying parched and yellow under the sunrise, and great cracks gaped in the earth as if it were thirsty. The trenches and channels were still there, but there was little water in them; and through the ragged fringes of the rusty vineyards I heard, instead of the cheerful songs of the vintagers, the creaking of dry windlasses and the hoarse throb of the pumps in sunken wells. The girdle of gardens had shrunk like a wreath of withered flowers, and all the bright embroidery of earth was faded to a sullen gray.

At the foot of an ancient, leafless olive-tree I saw a group of people kneeling around a newly opened well. I asked a man who was digging beside the dusty path what this might mean. He straightened himself for a moment, wiping the sweat from his brow, and answered, sullenly, "They are worshipping the windlass: how else should they bring water into their fields?" Then he fell furiously to digging again, and I passed on into the city.

There was no sound of murmuring streams in the streets, and down the main bed of the river I saw only a few shallow puddles, joined together by a slowly trickling thread. Even these were fenced and guarded so that no one might come near to them, and there were men going among the houses with water-skins on their shoulders, crying "Water! Water to sell!"

The marble pools in the open square were empty; and at one of them there was a crowd looking at a man who was being beaten with rods. A bystander told me that the officers of the city had ordered him to be punished because he had said that the pools and the basins and the channels were not all of pure marble, without a flaw. "For this," said he, "is the evil doctrine that has come in to take away the glory of our city, and because of this the water has failed."

"It is a sad change," I answered, "and doubtless they who have caused it should suffer more than others. But can you tell me at what hour and in what manner the people now observe the visitation of the Source?"

He looked curiously at me and replied: "I do not understand you. There is no visitation save the inspection of the cisterns and the wells which the syndics of the city, whom we call the Princes of Water, carry on daily at every hour. What source is this of which you speak?"

So I went on through the street, where all the passers-by seemed in haste and wore weary countenances, until I came to the house where I had lodged. There was a little basin here against the wall, with a slender stream of water still flowing into it, and a group of children standing near with their pitchers, waiting to fill them.

The door of the house was closed; but when I knocked, it opened and a maiden came forth. She was pale and sad in aspect, but a light of joy dawned over the snow of her face, and I knew by the youth in her eyes that it was Ruamie, who had walked with me through the vineyards long ago.

With both hands she welcomed me, saying: "You are expected. Have you found the Blue Flower?"

"Not yet," I answered, "but something drew me back to you. I would know how it fares with you, and I would go again with you to visit the Source."

At this her face grew bright, but with a tender, half-sad brightness.

"The Source!" she said. "Ah, yes, I was sure that you would remember it. And this is the hour of the visitation. Come, let us go up together."

Then we went alone through the busy and weary multitudes of the city toward the mountain-path. So forsaken was it and so covered with stones and overgrown with wire-grass that I could not have found it but for her guidance. But as we climbed upward the air grew clearer, and more sweet, and I questioned her of the things that had come to pass in my absence. I asked her of the kind old man who had taken me into his house when I came as a stranger. She said, softly, "He is dead."

"And where are the men and women, his friends, who once thronged this pathway? Are they also dead?"

"They also are dead."

"But where are the younger ones who sang here so gladly as they marched upward? Surely they are living?"

"They have forgotten."

"Where then are the young children whose fathers taught them this way and bade them remember it? Have they forgotten?"

"They have forgotten."

"But why have you alone kept the hour of visitation? Why have you not turned back with your companions? How have you walked here solitary day after day?"

She turned to me with a divine regard, and laying her hand gently over mine, she said, "I remember always."

Then I saw a few wild-flowers blossoming beside the path.

We drew near to the Source, and entered into the

chamber hewn in the rock. She kneeled and bent over the sleeping spring. She murmured again and again the beautiful name of him who had died to find it. Her voice repeated the song that had once been sung by many voices. Her tears fell softly on the spring, and as they fell it seemed as if the water stirred and rose to meet her bending face, and when she looked up it was as if the dew had fallen on a flower.

We came very slowly down the path along the river Carita, and rested often beside it, for surely, I thought, the rising of the spring had sent a little more water down its dry bed, and some of it must flow on to the city. So it was almost evening when we came back to the streets. The people were hurrying to and fro, for it was the day before the choosing of new Princes of Water; and there was much dispute about them, and strife over the building of new cisterns to hold the stores of rain which might fall in the next year. But none cared for us, as we passed by like strangers, and we came unnoticed to the door of the house.

Then a great desire of love and sorrow moved within my breast, and I said to Ruamie, "You are the life of the city, for you alone remember. Its secret is in your heart, and your faithful keeping of the hours of visitation is the only cause why the river has not failed altogether and the curse of desolation returned. Let me stay with you, sweet soul of all the flowers that are dead, and I will cherish you forever. Together we will visit the Source every day; and we shall turn the people, by our lives and by our words, back to that which they have forgotten."

There was a smile in her eyes so deep that its meaning cannot be spoken, as she lifted my hand to her lips, and answered,

"No so, dear friend, for who can tell whether life or death will come to the city, whether its people will remember at last, or whether they will forget forever. Its lot is mine, for I was born here, and here my life is rooted. But you are of the Children of the Unquiet Heart, whose feet can never rest until their task of errors is completed and their lesson of wandering is learned to the end. Until then go forth, and do not forget that I shall remember always."

Behind her quiet voice I heard the silent call that compels us, and passed down the street as one walking in a dream. At the place where the path turned aside to the ruined vineyards I looked back. The low sunset made a circle of golden rays about her head and a strange twin blossom of celestial blue seemed to shine in her tranquil eyes.

Since then I know not what has befallen the city, nor whether it is still called Saloma, or once more Ablis, which is Forsaken. But if it lives at all, I know that it is because there is one there who remembers, and keeps the hour of visitation, and treads the steep way, and breathes the beautiful name over the spring, and sometimes I think that long before my seeking and journeying brings me to the Blue Flower, it will bloom for Ruamie beside the still waters of the Source.

The Mill

The Mill

I

How the Young Martimor would Become a Knight and Assay Great Adventure

When Sir Lancelot was come out of the Red Launds where he did many deeds of arms, he rested him long with play and game in a land that is called Beausejour. For in that land there are neither castles nor enchantments, but many fair manors, with orchards and fields lying about them; and the people that dwell therein have good cheer continually.

Of the wars and of the strange quests that are ever afoot in Northgalis and Lionesse and the Out Isles, they hear nothing; but are well content to till the earth in summer when the world is green; and when the autumn changes green to gold they pitch pavilions among the fruit-trees and the vineyards, making merry with song and dance while they gather harvest of corn and apples and grapes; and in the white days of winter for pastime they have music of divers instruments and the playing of pleasant games.

But of the telling of tales in that land there is little skill, neither do men rightly understand the singing of ballads and romaunts. For one year there is like another, and so their life runs away, and they leave the world to God.

Then Sir Lancelot had great ease for a time in this quiet land, and often he lay under the apple-trees sleeping, and again he taught the people new games and feats of skill. For into what place soever he came he was welcome, though the inhabitants knew not his name and great renown, nor the famous deeds that he had done in tournament and battle. Yet for his own sake, because he was a very gentle knight, fair-spoken and full of courtesy and a good man of his hands withal, they doted upon him.

So he began to tell them tales of many things that have been done in the world by clean knights and faithful squires. Of the wars against the Saracens and misbelieving men; of the discomfiture of the Romans when they came to take truage of King Arthur; of the strife with the eleven kings and the battle that was ended but never finished; of the Questing Beast and how King Pellinore and then Sir Palamides followed it; of Balin that gave the dolourous stroke unto King Pellam; of Sir Tor that sought the lady's brachet and by the way overcame two knights and smote off the head of the outrageous caitiff Abelleus, —of these and many like matters of pith and moment, full of blood and honour, told Sir Lancelot, and the people had marvel of his words.

Now, among them that listened to him gladly, was a youth of good blood and breeding, very fair in the face and of great stature. His name was Martimor. Strong of arm was he, and his neck was like a pillar. His legs were as tough as beams of ash-wood, and in his heart was the hunger of noble tatches and deeds. So when he heard of Sir Lancelot these redoubtable histories he was taken with desire to assay his strength. And he besought the knight that they might joust together.

But in the land of Beausejour there were no arms of war save such as Sir Lancelot had brought with him. Wherefore they made shift to fashion a harness out of kitchen gear, with a brazen platter for a breast-plate, and the cover of the greatest of all kettles for a shield, and for a helmet a round pot of iron, whereof the handle stuck down at Martimor's back like a tail. And for spear he got him a stout young fir-tree, the point hardened in the fire, and Sir Lancelot lent to him the sword that he had taken from the false knight that distressed all ladies.

Thus was Martimor accoutred for the jousting, and when he had climbed upon his horse, there arose much laughter and mockage. Self Sir Lancelot laughed a little, though he was ever a grave man, and said, "Now must we call this knight, *La Queue de Fer,* by reason of the tail at his back."

But Martimor was half merry and half wroth, and crying " 'Ware!" he dressed his spear beneath his arm. Right so he rushed upon Sir Lancelot, and so marvellously did his harness jangle and smite together as he came, that the horse of Sir Lancelot was frighted and turned aside. Thus the point of the fir-tree caught him upon the shoulder and came near to unhorse him. Then Martimor drew rein and shouted: "Ha! ha! has Iron-Tail done well?"

"Nobly hast thou done," said Lancelot, laughing, the while he amended his horse, "but let not the first stroke turn thy head, else will the tail of thy helmet hang down afore thee and mar the second stroke!"

So he kept his horse in hand and guided him warily, making feint now on this side and now on that, until he was aware that the youth grew hot with the joy of fighting and sought to deal with him roughly and bigly. Then he cast aside his spear and drew sword, and as Martimor walloped toward him, he lightly swerved, and with one stroke cut in twain the young fir-tree, so that not above an ell was left in the youth's hand.

Then was the youth full of fire, and he also drew sword and made at Sir Lancelot, lashing heavily as he would hew down a tree. But the knight guarded and warded without distress, until the other breathed hard and was blind with sweat. Then Lancelot smote him with a mighty stroke upon the head, but with the flat of his sword, so that Martimor's breath went clean out of him, and the blood gushed from his mouth, and he fell over the croup of his horse as he were a man slain.

Then Sir Lancelot laughed no more, but grieved, for he weened that he had harmed the youth, and he liked him passing well. So he ran to him and held him in his arms fast and tended him. And when the breath came again into his body, Lancelot was glad, and desired the youth that he would pardon him of that unequal joust and of the stroke too heavy.

At this Martimor sat up and took him by the hand.

"Pardon?" he cried. "No talk of pardon between thee and me, my Lord Lancelot! Thou hast given me such joy of my life as never I had before. It made me glad to feel thy might. And now am I delibred and fully concluded that I also will become a knight, and thou shalt instruct me how and in what land I shall seek great adventure."

II

How Martimor was Instructed of Sir Lancelot to Set Forth Upon His Quest

So right gladly did Sir Lancelot advise the young Martimor of all the customs and vows of the noble order of knighthood, and shew how he might become a well-ruled and a hardy knight to win good fame and renown. For between these two from the first there was close brotherhood and affiance, though in years and in breeding they were so far apart, and this brotherhood endured until the last, as ye shall see, nor was the affiance broken.

Thus willingly learned the youth of his master; being instructed first in the art and craft to manage and guide a horse; then to handle the shield and the spear, and both to cut and to foin with the sword; and last of all in the laws of honour and courtesy, whereby a man may rule his own spirit and so obtain grace of God, praise of princes, and favour of fair ladies.

"For this I tell thee," said Sir Lancelot, as they sat together under an apple-tree, "there be many good fighters that are false knights, breaking faith with man and woman, envious, lustful and orgulous. In them courage is cruel, and love is lecherous. And in the end they shall come to shame and shall be overcome by a simpler knight than themselves; or else they shall win sorrow and despite by the slaying of better men than they be; and with their paramours they shall have weary dole and distress of soul and body; for he that is false, to him shall none be true, but all things shall be unhappy about him."

"But how and if a man be true in heart," said Martimor, "yet by some enchantment, or evil fortune, he may do an ill deed and one that is harmful to his lord or to his friend, even as Balin and his brother Balan slew each the other unknown?"

"That is in God's hand," said Lancelot. "Doubtless he may pardon and assoil all such in their unhappiness, forasmuch as the secret of it is with him."

"And how if a man be entangled in love," said Martimor, "yet his love be set upon one that is not lawful for him to have? For either he must deny his love, which is great shame, or else he must do dishonour to the law. What shall he then do?"

At this Sir Lancelot was silent, and heaved a great sigh. Then said he: "Rest assured that this man shall have sorrow enough. For out of this net he may not escape, save by falsehood on the one side, or by treachery on the other. Therefore say I that he shall not assay to escape, but rather right manfully to bear the bonds with which he is bound, and to do honour to them."

"How may this be?" said Martimor.

"By clean living," said Lancelot, "and by keeping himself from wine which heats the blood, and by quests and labours and combats wherein the fierceness of the heart is spent and overcome, and by inward joy in the pure worship of his lady, whereat none may take offence."

"How then shall a man bear himself in the following of a quest?" said Martimor. "Shall he set his face ever forward, and turn not to right, or left, whatever meet him by the way? Or shall he hold himself ready to answer them that call to him, and to succour them that ask help of him, and to turn aside from his path for rescue and good service?"

"Enough of questions!" said Lancelot. "These are things whereto each man must answer for himself, and not for other. True knight taketh counsel of the time. Every day his own deed. And the winning of a quest is not by haste, nor by hap, but what needs to be done, that must ye do while ye are in the way."

Then because of the love that Sir Lancelot bore to Martimor he gave him his own armour, and the good spear wherewith he had unhorsed many knights, and the

sword that he took from Sir Peris de Forest Savage that
distressed all ladies, but his shield he gave not, for therein
his own remembrance was blazoned. So he let make a
new shield, and in the corner was painted a Blue Flower
that was nameless, and this he gave to Martimor, saying: "Thou shalt name it when thou hast found it, and so
shalt thou have both crest and motto."

"Now am I well beseen," cried Martimor, "and my
adventures are before me. Which way shall I ride, and
where shall I find them?"

"Ride into the wind," said Lancelot, "and what chance
soever it blows thee, thereby do thy best, as it were the
first and the last. Take not thy hand from it until it be
fulfilled. So shalt thou most quickly and worthily achieve
knighthood."

Then they embraced like brothers; and each bade other
keep him well; and Sir Lancelot in leather jerkin, with
naked head, but with his shield and sword, rode to the
south toward Camelot; and Martimor rode into the wind,
westward, over the hill.

III
How Martimor Came to the Mill and There was
Stayed in a Delay

So by wildsome ways in strange countries and through
many waters and valleys rode Martimor forty days,
but adventure met him none, blow the wind never so
fierce or fickle. Neither dragons, nor giants, nor false
knights, nor distressed ladies, nor fays, nor kings im-
prisoned could he find.

"These are ill times for adventure," said he, "the world
is full of meat and sleepy. Now must I ride farther afield
and undertake some ancient, famous quest wherein other
knights have failed and fallen. Either I shall follow the
Questing Beast with Sir Palamides, or I shall find Mer-
lin at the great stone whereunder the Lady of the Lake
enchanted him and deliver him from that enchantment,
or I shall assay the cleansing of the Forest Perilous, or

I shall win the favour of La Belle Dame Sans Merci, or mayhap I shall adventure the quest of the Sangreal. One or other of these will I achieve, or bleed the best blood of my body." Thus pondering and dreaming he came by the road down a gentle hill with close woods on either hand; and so into a valley with a swift river flowing through it; and on the river a Mill.

So white it stood among the trees, and so merrily whirred the wheel as the water turned it, and so bright blossomed the flowers in the garden, that Martimor had joy of the sight, for it minded him of his own country. "But here is no adventure," thought he, and made to ride by.

Even then came a young maid suddenly through the garden crying and wringing her hands. And when she saw him she cried him help. At this Martimor alighted quickly and ran into the garden, where the young maid soon led him to the millpond, which was great and deep, and made him understand that her little hound was swept away by the water and was near to perishing.

There saw he a red and white brachet, caught by the swift stream that ran into the race, fast swimming as ever he could swim, yet by no means able to escape. Then Martimor stripped off his harness and leaped into the water and did marvellously to rescue the little hound. But the fierce river dragged his legs, and buffeted him, and hurtled at him, and drew him down, as it were an enemy wrestling with him, so that he had much ado to come where the brachet was, and more to win back again, with the brachet in his arm, to the dry land.

Which when he had done he was clean for-spent and fell upon the ground as a dead man. At this the young maid wept yet more bitterly than she had wept for her hound, and cried aloud, "Alas, if so goodly a man should spend his life for my little brachet!" So she took his head upon her knee and cherished him and beat the palms of his hands, and the hound licked his face. And when Martimor opened his eyes he saw the face of the maid that it was fair as any flower.

Then was she shamed, and put him gently from her knee, and began to thank him and to ask with what she might reward him for the saving of the brachet.

"A night's lodging and a day's cheer," quoth Martimor.

"As long as thee liketh," said she, "for my father, the miller, will return ere sundown, and right gladly will he have a guest so brave."

"Longer might I like," said he, "but longer may I not stay, for I ride in a quest and seek great adventures to become a knight."

So they bestowed the horse in the stable, and went into the Mill; and when the miller was come home they had such good cheer with eating of venison and pan-cakes, and drinking of hydromel, and singing of pleasant ballads, that Martimor clean forgot he was in a delay. And going to his bed in a fair garret he dreamed of the Maid of the Mill, whose name was Lirette.

IV
How the Mill was in Danger and the Delay Endured

In the morning Martimor lay late and thought large thoughts of his quest, and whither it might lead him, and to what honour it should bring him. As he dreamed thus, suddenly he heard in the hall below a trampling of feet and a shouting, with the voice of Lirette crying and shrieking. With that he sprang out of his bed, and caught up his sword and dagger, leaping lightly and fiercely down the stair.

There he saw three foul churls, whereof two strove with the miller, beating him with great clubs, while the third would master the Maid and drag her away to do her shame, but she fought shrewdly. Then Martimor rushed upon the churls, shouting for joy, and there was a great medley of breaking chairs and tables and cursing and smiting, and with his sword he gave horrible strokes.

One of the knaves that fought with the miller, he smote upon the shoulder and clave him to the navel. And at

the other he foined fiercely so that the point of the sword
went through his back and stuck fast in the wall. But the
third knave, that was the biggest and the blackest, and
strove to bear away the Maid, left hold of her, and leaped
upon Martimor and caught him by the middle and
crushed him so that his ribs cracked.

Thus they weltered and wrung together, and now one
of them was above and now the other; and ever as they
wallowed Martimor smote him with his dagger, but there
came forth no blood, only water.

Then the black churl broke away from him and ran
out at the door of the mill, and Martimor after. So they
ran through the garden to the river, and there the churl
sprang into the water, and swept away raging and foaming. And as he went he shouted, "Yet will I put thee to the
worse, and mar the Mill, and have the Maid!"

Then Martimor cried, "Never while I live shalt thou
mar the Mill or have the Maid, thou foul, black, misbe-
gotten churl!" So he returned to the Mill, and there the
damsel Lirette made him to understand that these three
churls were long time enemies of the Mill, and sought
ever to destroy it and to do despite to her and her father.
One of them was Ignis, and another was Ventus, and
these were the twain that he had smitten. But the third,
that fled down the river(and he was ever the fiercest and
the most outrageous), his name was Flumen, for he dwelt
in the caves of the stream, and was the master of it before the Mill was built.

"And now," wept the Maid, "he must have had his will
with me and with the Mill, but for God's mercy, thanked
be our Lord Jesus!"

"Thank me too," said Martimor.

"So I do," said Lirette, and she kissed him. "Yet am I
heavy at heart and fearful, for my father is sorely mishandled and his arm is broken, so that he cannot tend
the Mill nor guard it. And Flumen is escaped; surely he
will harm us again. Now I know not, where I shall look
for help."

"Why not here?" said Martimor.

Then Lirette looked him in the face, smiling a little

sorrily. "But thou ridest in a quest," quoth she, "thou mayst not stay from thy adventures."

"A month," said he.

"Till my father be well?" said she.

"A month," said he.

"Till thou hast put Flumen to the worse?" said she.

"Right willingly would I have to do with that base, slippery knave again," said he, "but more than a month I may not stay, for my quest calls me and I must win worship of men or ever I become a knight."

So they bound up the miller's wounds and set the Mill in order. But Martimor had much to do to learn the working of the Mill; and they were busied with the grinding of wheat and rye and barley and divers kinds of grain; and the miller's hurts were mended every day; and at night there was merry rest and good cheer; and Martimor talked with the Maid of the great adventure that he must find; and thus the delay endured in pleasant wise.

V
Yet More of the Mill, and of the Same Delay, also of the Maid

Now at the end of the third month, which was November, Martimor made Lirette to understand that it was high time he should ride farther to follow his quest. For the miller was now recovered, and it was long that they had heard and seen naught of Flumen, and doubtless that black knave was well routed and dismayed that he would not come again. Lirette prayed him and desired him that he would tarry yet one week. But Martimor said, No! for his adventures were before him, and that he could not be happy save in the doing of great deeds and the winning of knightly fame. Then he showed her the Blue Flower in his shield that was nameless, and told her how Sir Lancelot had said that he must find it, then should he name it and have both crest and motto.

"Does it grow in my garden?" said Lirette.

"I have not seen it," said he, "and now the flowers are all faded."

"Perhaps in the month of May?" said she.

"In that month I will come again," said he, "for by that time it may fortune that I shall achieve my quest, but now forth must I fare."

So there was sad cheer in the Mill that day, and at night there came a fierce storm with howling wind and plumping rain, and Martimor slept ill. About the break of day he was wakened by a great roaring and pounding; then he looked out of window, and saw the river in flood, with black waves spuming and raving, like wood beasts, and driving before them great logs and broken trees. Thus the river hurled and hammered at the mill-dam so that it trembled, and the logs leaped as they would spring over it, and the voice of Flumen shouted hoarsely and hungrily, "Yet will I mar the Mill and have the Maid!"

Then Martimor ran with the miller out upon the dam, and they laboured at the gates that held the river back, and thrust away the logs that were heaped over them, and cut with axes, and fought with the river. So at last two of the gates were lifted and one was broken, and the flood ran down ramping and roaring in great raundon, and as it ran the black face of Flumen sprang above it, crying, "Yet will I mar both Mill and Maid."

"That shalt thou never do," cried Martimor, "by foul or fair, while the life beats in my body."

So he came back with the miller into the Mill, and there was meat ready for them and they ate strongly and with good heart. "Now," said the miller, "must I mend the gate. But how it may be done, I know not, for surely this will be great travail for a man alone."

"Why alone?" said Martimor.

"Thou wilt stay, then?" said Lirette.

"Yea," said he.

"For another month?" said she.

"Till the gate be mended," said he.

But when the gate was mended there came another flood and brake the second gate. And when that was mended there came another flood and brake the third gate. So when all three were mended firm and fast, being bound with iron, still the grimly river hurled over the dam, and the voice of Flumen muttered in the dark of winter nights, "Yet will I mar—mar—mar—yet will I mar Mill and Maid."

"Oho!" said Martimor, "this is a durable and dogged knave. Art thou feared of him Lirette?"

"Not so," said she, "for thou art stronger. But fear have I of the day when thou ridest forth in thy quest."

"Well, as to that," said he, "when I have overcome this false devil Flumen, then will we consider and appoint that day."

So the delay continued, and Martimor was both busy and happy at the Mill, for he liked and loved this damsel well, and was fain of her company. Moreover the strife with Flumen was great joy to him.

VI
How the Month of May came to the Mill, and the Delay was Made Longer

Now when the month of May came to the Mill it brought a plenty of sweet flowers, and Lirette wrought in the garden. With her, when the day was spent and the sun rested upon the edge of the hill, went Martimor, and she showed him all her flowers that were blue. But none of them was like the flower on his shield.

"Is it this?" she cried, giving him a violet.

"Too dark," said he.

"Then here it is," she said, plucking a posy of forget-me-not.

"Too light," said he.

"Surely this is it," and she brought him a spray of blue-bells.

"Too slender," said he, "and well I ween that I may not find that flower, till I ride farther in my quest and achieve great adventure."

Then was the Maid cast down, and Martimor was fain to comfort her.

So while they walked thus in the garden, the days were fair and still, and the river ran lowly and slowly, as it were full of gentleness, and Flumen had amended him of his evil ways. But full of craft and guile was that false foe. For now that the gates were firm and strong, he found a way down through the corner of the dam, where a water-rat had burrowed, and there the water went seeping and creeping, gnawing ever at the hidden breach. Presently in the night came a mizzling rain, and far among the hills a cloud brake open, and the mill-pond flowed over and under, and the dam crumbled away, and the Mill shook, and the whole river ran roaring through the garden.

Then was Martimor wonderly wroth, because the river had blotted out the Maid's flowers. "And one day," she cried, holding fast to him and trembling, "one day Flumen will have me, when thou art gone."

"Not so," said he, "by the faith of my body that foul fiend shall never have thee. I will bind him, I will compel him, or die in the deed."

So he went forth, upward along the river, till he came to a strait place among the hills. There was a great rock full of caves and hollows, and there the water whirled and burbled in furious wise. "Here," thought he, "is the hold of the knave Flumen, and if I may cut through above this rock and make a dyke with a gate in it, to let down the water another way when the floods come, so shall I spoil him of his craft and put him to the worse."

Then he toiled day and night to make the dyke, and ever by night Flumen came and strove with him, and did his power to cast him down and strangle him. But Martimor stood fast and drave him back.

And at last, as they wrestled and whapped together, they fell headlong in the stream.

"Ho-o!" shouted Flumen, "now will I drown thee, and mar the Mill and the Maid,"

But Martimor gripped him by the neck and thrust his head betwixt the leaves of the gate and shut them fast, so that his eyes stood out like gobbets of foam, and his black tongue hung from his mouth like a water-weed.

"Now shalt thou swear never to mar Mill nor Maid, but meekly to serve them," cried Martimor.

Then Flumen sware by wind and wave, by storm and stream, by rain and river, by pond and pool, by flood and fountain, by dyke and dam.

"These be changeable things," said Martimor, "swear by the Name of God."

So he sware, and even as the Name passed his teeth, the gobbets of foam floated forth from the gate, and the water-weed writhed away with the stream, and the river flowed fair and softly, with a sound like singing.

Then Martimor came back to the Mill, and told how Flumen was overcome and made to swear a pact. Thus their hearts waxed light and jolly, and they kept that day as it were a love-day.

VII

How Martimor Bled for a Lady and Lived for a Maid, and how His Great Adventure Ended and Began at the Mill

Now leave we of the Mill and Martimor and the Maid, and let us speak of a certain Lady, passing tall and fair and young. This was the Lady Beauvivante, that was daughter to King Pellinore. And three false knights took her by craft from her father's court and led her away to work their will on her. But she escaped from them as they slept by a well, and came riding on a white palfrey, over hill and dale, as fast as ever she could drive.

Thus she came to the Mill, and her palfrey was spent, and there she took refuge, beseeching Martimor that he would hide her, and defend her from those caitiff knights that must soon follow.

"Of hiding," said he, "will I hear naught, but of defending am I full fain. For this have I waited."

Then he made ready his horse and his armour, and took both spear and sword, and stood forth in the bridge. Now this bridge was strait, so that none could pass there but singly, and that not till Martimor yielded or was beaten down.

Then came the three knights that followed the Lady, riding fiercely down the hill. And when they came about ten spear-lengths from the bridge, they halted, and stood still as it had been a plump of wood. One rode in black, and one rode in yellow, and the third rode in black and yellow. So they cried Martimor that he should give them passage, for they followed a quest.

"Passage takes, who passage makes!" cried Martimor. "Right well I know your quest, and it is a foul one."

Then the knight in black rode at him lightly, but Martimor encountered him with the spear and smote him backward from his horse, that his head struck the coping of the bridge and brake his neck. Then came the knight in yellow, walloping heavily, and him the spear pierced through the midst of the body and burst in three pieces: so he fell on his back and the life went out of him, but the spear stuck fast and stood up from his breast as a stake.

Then the knight in black and yellow, that was as big as both his breathren, gave a terrible shout, and rode at Martimor like a wood lion. But he fended with his shield that the spear went aside, and they clapped together like thunder, and both horses were overthrown. And lightly they avoided their horses and rushed together, tracing, rasing, and foining. Such strokes they gave that great pieces were clipped away from their hauberks, and their helms, and they staggered to and fro like drunken men. Then they hurtled together like rams and each battered other the wind out of his body. So they sat either on one side of the bridge, to take their breath, glaring the one at the other as two owls. Then they stepped together and fought freshly, smiting and thrusting, ramping and reeling, panting, snorting, and scattering blood, for the space of two hours. So the knight in black and yellow, because he was heavier, drave Martimor backward step by step till he came to the crown of the bridge, and there fell grovelling. At this the Lady Beauvivante shrieked and wailed, but the damsel Lirette cried loudly, "Up! Martimor, strike again!"

Then the courage came into his body, and with a great might he abraid upon his feet, and smote the black and yellow knight upon the helm by an overstroke so fierce that the sword sheared away the third part of his head, as it had been a rotten cheese. So he lay upon the bridge, and the blood ran out of him. And Martimor smote off the rest of his head quite, and cast it into the river. Likewise did he with the other twain that lay dead beyond the bridge. And he cried to Flumen, "Hide me these black eggs that hatched evil thoughts." So the river bore them away.

Then Martimor came into the Mill, all for-bled; "Now are ye free, lady," he cried, and fell down in a swoon. Then the Lady and the Maid wept full sore and made great dole and unlaced his helm; and Lirette cherished him tenderly to recover his life.

So while they were thus busied and distressed, came Sir Lancelot with a great company of knights and squires riding for to rescue the princess. When he came to the bridge all bedashed with blood, and the bodies of the knights headless, "Now, by my lady's name," said he, "here has been good fighting, and those three caitiffs are slain! By whose hand I wonder?"

So he came into the Mill, and there he found Martimor recovered of his swoon, and had marvellous joy of him, when he heard how he had wrought.

"Now are thou proven worthy of the noble order of knighthood," said Lancelot, and forthwith he dubbed him knight.

Then he said that Sir Martimor should ride with him to the court of King Pellinore, to receive a castle and a fair lady to wife, for doubtless the King would deny him nothing to reward the rescue of his daughter.

But Martimor stood in a muse; then said he, "May a knight have his free will and choice of castles, where he will abide?"

"Within the law," said Lancelot, "and by the King's word he may."

"Then choose I the Mill," said Martimor, "for here will I dwell."

"Freely spoken," said Lancelot, laughing, "so art thou Sir Martimor of the Mill; no doubt the King will confirm it. And now what sayest thou of ladies?"

"May a knight have his free will and choice here also?" said he.

"According to his fortune," said Lancelot, "and by the lady's favour, he may."

"Well, then," said Sir Martimor, taking Lirette by the hand, "this Maid is to me liefer to have and to wield as my wife than any dame or princess that is christened."

"What, brother," said Sir Lancelot, "is the wind in that quarter? And will the Maid have thee?"

"I will well," said Lirette.

"Now are you well provided," said Sir Lancelot, "with knighthood, and a castle, and a lady. Lacks but a motto and a name for the Blue Flower in thy shield."

"He that names it shall never find it," said Sir Martimor, "and he that finds it needs no name."

So Lirette rejoiced Sir Martimor and loved together during their life-days; and this is the end and the beginning of the Story of the Mill.

A Handful of Clay

A Handful of Clay

There was a handful of clay in the bank of a river. It was only common clay, coarse and heavy; but it had high thoughts of its own value, and wonderful dreams of the great place which it was to fill in the world when the time came for its virtues to be discovered.

Overhead, in the spring sunshine, the trees whispered together of the glory which descended upon them when the delicate blossoms and leaves began to expand, and the forest glowed with fair, clear colours, as if the dust of thousands of rubies and emeralds were hanging, in soft clouds, above the earth.

The flowers, surprised with the joy of beauty, bent their heads to one another, as the wind caressed them, and said: "Sisters, how lovely you have become. You make the day bright."

The river, glad of new strength and rejoicing in the unison of all its waters, murmured to the shores in music, telling of its release from icy fetters, its swift flight from the snow-clad mountains, and the mighty work to which it was hurrying—the wheels of many mills to be turned, and great ships to be floated to the sea.

Waiting blindly in its bed, the clay comforted itself with lofty hopes. "My time will come," it said. "I was not made to be hidden forever. Glory and beauty and honour are coming to me in due season."

One day the clay felt itself taken from the place where it had waited so long. A flat blade of iron passed beneath it, and lifted it, and tossed it into a cart with other lumps of clay, and it was carried far away, as it seemed, over a rough and stony road. But it was not afraid, nor discouraged, for it said to itself: "This is necessary. The path to glory is always rugged. Now I am on my way to play a great part in the world."

But the hard journey was nothing compared with the tribulation and distress that came after it. The clay was put into a trough and mixed and beaten and stirred and trampled. It seemed almost unbearable. But there was consolation in the thought that something very fine and noble was certainly coming out of all this trouble. The clay felt sure that, if it could only wait long enough, a wonderful reward was in store for it.

Then it was put upon a swiftly turning wheel, and whirled around until it seemed as if it must fly into a thousand pieces. A strange power pressed it and moulded it, as it revolved, and through all the dizziness and pain it felt that it was taking a new form.

Then an unknown hand put it into an oven, and fires were kindled about it—fierce and penetrating—hotter than all the heats of summer that had ever brooded upon the bank of the river. But through all, the clay held itself together and endured its trials, in the confidence of a great future. "Surely," it thought, "I am intended for something very splendid, since such pains are taken with me. Perhaps I am fashioned for the ornament of a temple, or a precious vase for the table of a king."

At last the baking was finished. The clay was taken from the furnace and set down upon a board, in the cool air, under the blue sky. The tribulation was passed. The reward was at hand.

Close beside the board there was a pool of water, not very deep, nor very clear, but calm enough to reflect, with impartial truth, every image that fell upon it. There, for the first time, as it was lifted from the board, the clay saw its new shape, the reward of all its patience and pain, the consummation of its hopes—a common flower-pot, straight and stiff, red and ugly. And then it felt that it was not destined for a king's house, nor for a palace of art, because it was made without glory or beauty or honour; and it murmured against the unknown maker, saying, "Why hast thou made me thus?"

Many days it passed in sullen discontent. Then it was

filled with earth, and something—it knew not what—but something rough and brown and dead-looking, was thrust into the middle of the earth and covered over. The clay rebelled at this new disgrace. "This is the worst of all that has happened to me, to be filled with dirt and rubbish. Surely I am a failure."

But presently it was set in a greenhouse, where the sunlight fell warm upon it, and water was sprinkled over it, and day by day as it waited, a change began to come to it. Something was stirring within it—a new hope. Still it was ignorant, and knew not what the new hope meant.

One day the clay was lifted again from its place, and carried into a great church. Its dream was coming true after all. It had a fine part to play in the world. Glorious music flowed over it. It was surrounded with flowers. Still it could not understand. So it whispered to another vessel of clay, like itself, close beside it, "Why have they set me here? Why do all the people look toward us?" And the other vessel answered, "Do you not know? You are carrying a royal sceptre of lilies. Their petals are white as snow, and the heart of them is like pure gold. The people look this way because the flower is the most wonderful in the world. And the root of it is in your heart."

Then the clay was content, and silently thanked its maker, because, though an earthen vessel, it held so great a treasure.

A Brave Heart

A Brave Heart

"That was truly his name, m'sieu'—Raoul Vaillantcœur
—a name of the fine sound, is it not? You like that word,—
a valiant heart,—it pleases you, eh! The man who calls
himself by such a name as that ought to be a brave fellow,
a veritable hero? Well, perhaps. But I know an Indian
who is called Le Blanc; that means white. And a white
man who is called Lenoir; that means black. It is very
droll, this affair of the names. It is like the lottery."

Silence for a few moments, broken only by the ripple of
water under the bow of the canoe, the persistent patter
of the rain all around us, and the *slish, slish* of the paddle
with which Ferdinand, my Canadian voyageur, was pushing the birch-bark down the lonely length of Lac Moïse.
I knew that there was one of his stories on the way. But
I must keep still to get it. A single ill-advised comment,
a word that would raise a question of morals or social
philosophy, might switch the narrative off the track into
a swamp of abstract discourse in which Ferdinand would
lose himself. Presently the voice behind me began again.

"But that word *vaillant*, m'sieu'; with us in Canada it
does not mean always the same as with you. Sometimes
we use it for something that sounds big, but does little;
a gun that goes off with a terrible crack, but shoots not
straight nor far. When a man is like that he is *fanfaron*,
he shows off well, but—well, you shall judge for yourself,
when you hear what happened between this man Vaillantcœur and his friend Prosper Leclère at the building of the
stone tower of the church at Abbéville. You remind yourself of that grand church with the tall tower—yes? With
permission I am going to tell you what passed when that
was made. And you shall decide whether there was truly
a brave heart in the story, or not; and if it went with the
name."

Thus the tale began, in the vast solitude of the northern forest, among the granite peaks of the ancient Laurentian Mountains, on a lake that knew no human habitation save the Indian's wigwam or the fisherman's tent.

How it rained that day! The dark clouds had collapsed upon the hills in shapeless folds. The waves of the lake were beaten flat by the lashing strokes of the storm. Quivering sheets of watery gray were driven before the wind; and broad curves of silver bullets danced before them as they swept over the surface. All around the homeless shores the evergreen trees seemed to hunch their backs and crowd closer together in patient misery. Not a bird had the heart to sing; only the loon—storm-lover—laughed his crazy challenge to the elements, and mocked us with his long-drawn maniac scream.

It seemed as if we were a thousand miles from everywhere and everybody. Cities, factories, libraries, colleges, law-courts, theatres, palaces,—what had we dreamed of these things? They were far off, in another world. We had slipped back into a primitive life. Ferdinand was telling me the naked story of human love and human hate, even as it has been told from the beginning.

I cannot tell it just as he did. There was a charm in his speech too quick for the pen: a woodland savour not to be found in any ink for sale in the shops. I must tell it in my way, as he told it in his.

But at all events, nothing that makes any difference shall go into the translation unless it was in the original. This is Ferdinand's story. If you care for the real thing, here it is.

I

There were two young men in Abbéville who were easily the cocks of the woodland walk. Their standing rested on the fact that they were the strongest men in the parish. Strength is the thing that counts, when people live on the edge of the wilderness. These two were well known all through the country between Lake St. John and Chicoutimi as men of great capacity. Either of them could shoulder a barrel of flour and walk off with it as lightly as a common man would carry a side of bacon. There was not a half-pound of difference between them in ability. But there was a great difference in their looks and in their way of doing things.

Raoul Vaillantcœur was the biggest and the handsomest man in the village; nearly six feet tall, straight as a fir tree, and black as a bull-moose in December. He had natural force enough and to spare. Whatever he did was done by sheer power of back and arm. He could send a canoe up against the heaviest water, provided he did not get mad and break his paddle—which he often did. He had more muscle than he knew how to use.

Prosper Leclère did not have so much, but he knew better how to handle it. He never broke his paddle—unless it happened to be a bad one, and then he generally had another all ready in the canoe. He was at least four inches shorter than Vaillantcœur; broad shoulders, long arms, light hair, gray eyes; not a handsome fellow, but pleasant-looking and very quiet. What he did was done more than half with his head.

He was the kind of a man that never needs more than one match to light a fire.

But Vaillantcœur—well, if the wood was wet he might use a dozen, and when the blaze was kindled, as like as not he would throw in the rest of the box.

Now, these two men had been friends and were changed into rivals. At least that was the way that one of them looked at it. And most of the people in the parish seemed to think that was the right view.

It was a strange thing, and not altogether satisfactory to the public mind, to have *two* strongest men in the village. The question of comparative standing in the community ought to be raised and settled in the usual way. Raoul was perfectly willing, and at times (commonly on Saturday nights) very eager. But Prosper was not.

"No," he said, one March night, when he was boiling maple-sap in the sugar-bush with little Ovide Rossignol (who had a lyric passion for holding the coat while another man was fighting)—"no, for what shall I fight with Raoul? As boys we have played together. Once, in the rapids of the Belle Rivière, when I have fallen in the water, I think he has saved my life. He was stronger, then, than me. I am always a friend to him. If I beat him now, am I stronger? No, but weaker. And if he beats me, what is the sense of that? Certainly I shall not like it. What is to gain?"

Down in the store of old Girard, that night, Vaillant-cœur was holding forth after a different fashion. He stood among the cracker-boxes and flour-barrels, with a background of shelves laden with bright-coloured calicoes, and a line of tin pails hanging overhead, and stated his view of the case with vigour. He even pulled off his coat and rolled up his shirt-sleeve to show the knotty arguments with which he proposed to clinch his opinion.

"That Leclère," said he, "that little Prosper Leclère! He thinks himself one of the strongest—a fine fellow! But I tell you he is a coward. If he is clever? Yes. But he is a poltroon. He knows well that I can flatten him out like a *crêpe* in the frying-pan. But he is afraid. He has not as much courage as the musk-rat. You stamp on the bank. He dives. He swims away. Bah!"

"How about that time he cut loose the jam of logs in the Rapide des Cèdres?" said old Girard from his corner.

Vaillantcœur's black eyes sparkled and he twirled his mustache fiercely. "*Saprie!*" he cried, "that was nothing! Any man with an axe can cut a log. But to fight—that is another affair. That demands the brave heart. The strong man who will not fight is a coward. Some day I will put him through the mill—you shall see what that small Leclère is made of. *Sacrédam!*"

Of course, affairs had not come to this pass all at once. It was a long history, beginning with the time when the two boys had played together, and Raoul was twice as strong as the other, and was very proud of it. Prosper did not care; it was all right so long as they had a good time. But then Prosper began to do things better and better. Raoul did not understand it; he was jealous. Why should he not always be the leader? He had more force. Why should Prosper get ahead? Why should he have better luck at the fishing and the hunting and the farming? It was by some trick. There was no justice in it.

Raoul was not afraid of anything but death; and whatever he wanted, he thought he had a right to have. But he did not know very well how to get it. He would start to chop a log just at the spot where there was a big knot.

He was the kind of a man that sets hare-snares on a caribou-trail, and then curses his luck because he catches nothing.

Besides, whatever he did, he was always thinking most about beating somebody else. But Prosper cared most for doing the thing as well as he could. If any one else could beat him—well, what difference did it make? He would do better the next time.

If he had a log to chop, he looked it all over for a clear place before he began. What he wanted was, not to make the chips fly, but to get the wood split.

You are not to suppose that the one man was a saint and a hero, and the other a fool and a ruffian. No; that sort of thing happens only in books. People in Abbéville were not made on that plan. They were both plain men. But there was a difference in their hearts; and out of that difference grew all the trouble.

It was hard on Vaillantcœur, of course, to see Leclère going ahead, getting rich, clearing off the mortgage on his farm, laying up money with the notary Bergeron, who acted as banker for the parish—it was hard to look on at this, while he himself stood still, or even slipped back a little, got into debt, had to sell a bit of the land that his father left him. There must be some cheating about it.

But this was not the hardest morsel to swallow. The great thing that stuck in his crop was the idea that the little Prosper, whom he could have whipped so easily, and whom he had protected so loftily, when they were boys, now stood just as high as he did as a capable man —perhaps even higher. Why was it that when the Price Brothers, down at Chicoutimi, had a good lumber-job up in the woods on the Belle Rivière, they made Leclère the boss, instead of Vaillantcœur? Why did the curé Villeneuve choose Prosper, and not Raoul, to steady the strain of the biggest pole when they were setting up the derrick for the building of the new church?

It was rough, rough! The more Raoul thought of it, the rougher it seemed. The fact that it was a man who had once been his *protégé*, and still insisted on being his best friend, did not make it any smoother. Would you have liked it any better on that account? I am not telling you how it ought to have been, I am telling you how it was. This isn't Vaillantcœur's account-book; it's his story. You must strike your balances as you go along.

And all the time, you see, he felt sure that he was a stronger man and a braver man than Prosper. He was hungry to prove it in the only way that he could understand. The sense of rivalry grew into a passion of hatred, and the hatred shaped itself into a blind, headstrong desire to fight. Everything that Prosper did well, seemed like a challenge; every success that he had was as hard to bear as an insult. All the more, because Prosper seemed unconscious of it. He refused to take offence, went about his work quietly and cheerfully, turned off hard words with a joke, went out of his way to show himself friendly and good-natured. In reality, of course, he knew well enough how matters stood. But he was resolved not to show that he knew, if he could help it; and in any event, not to be one of the two that are needed to make a quarrel.

He felt very strangely about it. There was a presentiment in his heart that he did not dare to shake off. It seemed as if this conflict were one that would threaten the happiness of his whole life. He still kept his old feeling of attraction to Raoul, the memory of the many happy days they had spent together; and though the friendship, of course, could never again be what it had been, there was something of it left, at least on Prosper's side. To struggle with this man, strike at his face, try to maim and disfigure him, roll over and over on the ground with him, like two dogs tearing each other,—the thought was hateful. His gorge rose at it. He would never do it, unless to save his life. Then? Well, then, God must be his judge.

So it was that these two men stood against each other

in Abbéville. Just as strongly as Raoul was set to get into a fight, just so strongly was Prosper set to keep out of one. It was a trial of strength between two passions,— the passion of friendship and the passion of fighting.

Two or three things happened to put an edge on Raoul's hunger for an out-and-out fight.

The first was the affair at the shanty on Lac des Caps. The wood-choppers, like sailors, have a way of putting a new man through a few tricks to initiate him into the camp. Leclère was bossing the job, with a gang of ten men from St. Raymond under him. Vaillantcœur had just driven a team in over the snow with a load of provisions, and was lounging around the camp as if it belonged to him. It was Sunday afternoon, the regular time for fun, but no one dared to take hold of him. He looked too big. He expressed his opinion of the camp.

"No fun in this shanty, *hé*? I suppose that little Leclère he makes you others work, and say your prayers, and then, for the rest, you can sleep. *Hé*! Well, I am going to make a little fun for you, my boys. Come, Prosper, get your hat, if you are able to climb a tree."

He snatched the hat from the table by the stove and ran out into the snow. In front of the shanty a good-sized birch, tall, smooth, very straight, was still standing. He went up the trunk like a bear.

But there was a dead balsam that had fallen against the birch and lodged on the lower branches. It was barely strong enough to bear the weight of a light man. Up this slanting ladder Prosper ran quickly in his moccasined feet, snatched the hat from Raoul's teeth as he swarmed up the trunk, and ran down again. As he neared the ground, the balsam, shaken from its lodgement, cracked and fell. Raoul was left up the tree, perched among the branches, out of breath. Luck had set the scene for the lumberman's favourite trick.

"Chop him down! chop him down!" was the cry; and a trio of axes were twanging against the birch tree, while the other men shouted and laughed and pelted the tree with ice to keep the prisoner from climbing down.

Prosper neither shouted nor chopped, but he grinned

a little as he watched the tree quiver and shake, and heard the rain of "*sacrés!*" and "*maudits!*" that came out of the swaying top. He grinned—until he saw that a half-dozen more blows would fell the birch right on the roof of the shanty.

"Are you crazy?" he cried, as he picked up an axe; "you know nothing how to chop. You kill a man. You smash the *cabane*. Let go!" He shoved one of the boys away and sent a few mighty cuts into the side of the birch that was farthest from the cabin; then two short cuts on the other side; the tree shivered, staggered, cracked, and swept in a great arc toward the deep snow-drift by the brook. As the top swung earthward, Raoul jumped clear of the crashing branches and landed safely in the feather-bed of snow, buried up to his neck. Nothing was to be seen of him but his head, like some new kind of fire-work—sputtering bad words.

Well, this was the first thing that put an edge on Vaillantcœur's hunger to fight. No man likes to be chopped down by his friend, even if the friend does it for the sake of saving him from being killed by a fall on the shanty-roof. It is easy to forget that part of it. What you remember is the grin.

The second thing that made it worse was the bad chance that both of these men had to fall in love with the same girl. Of course there were other girls in the village beside Marie Antoinette Girard—plenty of them, and good girls, too. But somehow or other, when they were beside her, neither Raoul nor Prosper cared to look at any of them, but only at 'Toinette. Her eyes were so much darker and her cheeks so much more red—bright as the berries of the mountain-ash in September. Her hair hung down to her waist on Sunday in two long braids, brown and shiny like a ripe hazelnut; and her voice when she laughed made the sound of water tumbling over little stones.

No one knew which of the two lovers she liked best. At school it was certainly Raoul, because he was bigger and bolder. When she came back from her year in the convent at Roberval it was certainly Prosper, because he could talk better and had read more books. He had a volume of songs full of love and romance, and knew most of them by heart. But this did not last forever. 'Toinette's manners had been polished at the convent, but her ideas were still those of her own people. She never thought that knowledge of books could take the place of strength, in the real battle of life. She was a brave girl, and she felt sure in her heart that the man of the most courage must be the best man after all.

For a while she appeared to persuade herself that it was Prosper, beyond a doubt, and always took his part when the other girls laughed at him. But this was not altogether a good sign. When a girl really loves, she does not talk, she acts. The current of opinion and gossip in the village was too strong for her. By the time of the affair of the "chopping-down" at Lac des Caps, her heart was swinging to and fro like a pendulum. One week she would walk home from mass with Raoul. The next week she would loiter in the front yard on a Saturday evening and talk over the gate with Prosper, until her father called her into the shop to wait on customers.

It was in one of these talks that the pendulum seemed to make its last swing and settle down to its resting-place. Prosper was telling her of the good crops of sugar that he had made from his maple grove.

"The profit will be large—more than sixty piastres—and with that I shall buy at Chicoutimi a new four-wheeler, of the finest, a veritable wedding-carriage—if you—if I— 'Toinette? Shall we ride together?"

His left hand clasped hers as it lay on the gate. His right arm stole over the low picket fence and went around the shoulder that leaned against the gate-post. The road was quite empty, the night already dark. He could feel her warm breath on his neck as she laughed.

"If you! If I! If what? Why so many ifs in this fine speech? Of whom is the wedding for which this new carriage is to be bought? Do you know what Raoul Vaillant-cœur has said? 'No more wedding in this parish till I have thrown the little Prosper over my shoulder!' "

As she said this, laughing, she turned closer to the

fence and looked up, so that a curl on her forehead brushed against his cheek.

"*Batêche!* Who told you he said that?"

"I heard him, myself."

"Where?"

"In the store, two nights ago. But it was not for the first time. He said it when we came from the church together, it will be four weeks to-morrow."

"What did you say to him?"

"I told him perhaps he was mistaken. The next wedding might be after the little Prosper had measured the road with the back of the longest man in Abbéville."

The laugh had gone out of her voice now. She was speaking eagerly, and her bosom rose and fell with quick breaths. But Prosper's right arm had dropped from her shoulder, and his hand gripped the fence as he straightened up.

" 'Toinette!" he cried, "that was bravely said. And I could do it. Yes, I know I could do it. But, *mon Dieu*, what shall I say? Three years now, he has pushed me, every one has pushed me, to fight. And you—but I cannot. I am not capable of it."

The girl's hand lay in his as cold and still as a stone. She was silent for a moment, and then asked, coldly, "Why not?"

"Why not? Because of the old friendship. Because he pulled me out of the river long ago. Because I am still his friend. Because now he hates me too much. Because it would be a black fight. Because shame and evil would come of it, whoever won. That is what I fear, 'Toinette!"

Her hand slipped suddenly away from his. She stepped back from the gate.

"*Tiens!* You have fear, Monsieur Leclère! Truly? I had not thought of that. It is strange. For so strong a man it is a little stupid to be afraid. Goodnight. I hear my father calling me. Perhaps some one in the store who wants to be served. You must tell me again what you are going to do with the new carriage. Good-night!"

She was laughing again. But it was a different laughter. Prosper, at the gate, did not think it sounded like the running of a brook over the stones. No, it was more the noise of the dry branches that knock together in the wind. He did not hear the sigh that came as she shut the door of the house, nor see how slowly she walked through the passage into the store.

II

There seemed to be a great many rainy Saturdays that spring; and in the early summer the trade in Girard's store was so brisk that it appeared to need all the force of the establishment to attend to it. The gate of the front yard had no more strain put upon its hinges. It fell into a stiff propriety of opening and shutting, at the touch of people who understood that a gate was made merely to pass through, not to lean upon.

That summer Vaillantcœur had a new hat—a black and shiny beaver—and a new red-silk cravat. They looked fine on Corpus Christi day, when he and 'Toinette walked together as fiancées.

You would have thought he would have been content with that. Proud, he certainly was. He stepped like the curé's big rooster with the topknot—almost as far up in the air as he did along the ground; and he held his chin high, as if he liked to look at things over his nose.

But he was not satisfied all the way through. He thought more of beating Prosper than of getting 'Toinette. And he was not quite sure that he had beaten him yet.

Perhaps the girl still liked Prosper a little. Perhaps she still thought of his romances, and his *chansons*, and his fine, smooth words, and missed them. Perhaps she was too silent and dull sometimes, when she walked with Raoul; and sometimes she laughed too loud when he talked, more at him than with him. Perhaps those St. Raymond fellows still remembered the way his head stuck out of that cursed snow-drift, and joked about it, and said how clever and quick the little Prosper was. Perhaps—ah, *maudit!* a thousand times perhaps! And only one way to settle them, the old way, the sure way, and all the better now because 'Toinette must be on his side. She must understand for sure that the bravest man in the parish had chosen her.

That was the summer of the building of the grand stone tower of the church. The men of Abbéville did it themselves, with their own hands, for the glory of God. They were keen about that, and the curé was the keenest of them all. No sharing of that glory with workmen from Quebec, if you please! Abbéville was only forty years old, but they already understood the glory of God quite as well there as at Quebec, without doubt. They could build their own tower, perfectly, and they would. Besides, it would cost less.

Vaillantcœur was the chief carpenter. He attended to the affair of beams and timbers. Leclère was the chief mason. He directed the affair of dressing the stones and laying them. That required a very careful head, you understand, for the tower must be straight. In the floor a little crookedness did not matter; but in the wall—that might be serious. People have been killed by a falling tower. Of course, if they were going into church, they would be sure of heaven. But then think—what a disgrace for Abbéville!

Every one was glad that Leclère bossed the raising of the tower. They admitted that he might not be brave, but he was assuredly careful. Vaillantcœur alone grumbled, and said the work went too slowly, and even swore that the sockets for the beams were too shallow, or else too deep, it made no difference which. That *bête* Prosper made trouble always by his poor work. But the friction never came to a blaze; for the curé was pottering about the tower every day and all day long, and a few words from him would make a quarrel go off in smoke.

"Softly, my boys!" he would say; "work smooth and you work fast. The logs in the river run well when they run all the same way. But when two logs cross each other, on the same rock—psst! a jam! The whole drive is hung up! Do not run crossways, my children."

The walls rose steadily, straight as a steamboat pipe— ten, twenty, thirty, forty feet; it was time to put in the two cross-girders, lay the floor of the belfry, finish off the stonework, and begin the pointed wooden spire. The curé had gone to Quebec that very day to buy the shining plates of tin for the roof, and a beautiful cross of gilt for the pinnacle.

Leclère was in front of the tower putting on his overalls. Vaillantcœur came up, swearing mad. Three or four other workmen were standing about.

"Look here, you Leclère," said he, "I tried one of the cross-girders yesterday afternoon and it wouldn't go. The templet on the north is crooked—crooked as your teeth. We had to let the girder down again. I suppose we must trim it off some way, to get a level bearing, and make the tower weak, just to match your *sacré* bad work, eh?"

"Well," said Prosper, pleasant and quiet enough, "I'm sorry for that, Raoul. Perhaps I could put that templet straight, or perhaps the girder might be a little warped and twisted, eh? What? Suppose we measure it."

Sure enough, they found the long timber was not half seasoned and had corkscrewed itself out of shape at least three inches. Vaillantcœur sat on the sill of the doorway and did not even look at them while they were measuring. When they called out to him what they had found, he strode over to them.

"It's a dam' lie," he said, sullenly. "Prosper Leclère, you slipped the string. None of your *sacré* cheating! I have enough of it already. Will you fight, you cursed sneak?"

Prosper's face went gray, like the mortar in the trough. His fists clenched and the cords on his neck stood out as if they were ropes. He breathed hard. But he only said three words:

"No! Not here."

"Not here? Why not? There is room. The curé is away. Why not here?"

"It is the house of *le bon Dieu*. Can we build it in hate?"

"*Polisson!* You make an excuse. Then come to Girard's, and fight there."

Again Prosper held in for a moment, and spoke three words:

"No! Not now."

"Not now? But when, you heart of a hare? Will you sneak out of it until you turn gray and die? When will you fight, little musk-rat?"

"When I have forgotten. When I am no more your friend."

Prosper picked up his trowel and went into the tower. Raoul bad-worded him and every stone of his building from foundation to cornice, and then went down the road to get a bottle of cognac.

An hour later he came back breathing out threatenings and slaughter, strongly flavoured with raw spirits. Prosper was working quietly on the top of the tower, at the side away from the road. He saw nothing until Raoul, climbing up by the ladders on the inside, leaped on the platform and rushed at him like a crazy lynx.

"Now!" he cried, "no hole to hide in here, rat! I'll squeeze the lies out of you."

He gripped Prosper by the head, thrusting one thumb into his eye, and pushing him backward on the scaffolding.

Blinded, half maddened by the pain, Prosper thought of nothing but to get free. He swung his long arm upward and landed a heavy blow on Raoul's face that dislocated the jaw; then twisting himself downward and sideways, he fell in toward the wall. Raoul plunged forward, stumbled, let go his hold, and pitched out from the tower, arms spread, clutching the air.

Forty feet straight down! A moment—or was it an eternity?—of horrible silence. Then the body struck the rough stones at the foot of the tower with a thick, soft dunt, and lay crumpled up among them, without a groan, without a movement.

When the other men, who had hurried up the ladders in terror, found Leclère, he was peering over the edge of the scaffold, wiping the blood from his eyes, trying to see down.

"I have killed him," he muttered, "my friend! He is

smashed to death. I am a murderer. Let me go. I must throw myself down!"

They had hard work to hold him back. As they forced him down the ladders he trembled like a popular.

But Vaillantcœur was not dead. No; it was incredible—to fall forty feet and not be killed—they talk of it yet all through the valley of the Lake St. John—it was a miracle! But Vaillantcœur had broken only a nose, a collar-bone, and two ribs—for one like him that was but a *bagatelle*. A good doctor from Chicoutimi, a few months of nursing, and he would be on his feet again, almost as good a man as he had ever been.

It was Leclère who put himself in charge of this.

"It is my affair," he said—"my fault! It was not a fair place to fight. Why did I strike? I must attend to this bad work."

"Mais, sacré bleu!" they answered, "how could you help it? He forced you. You did not want to be killed. That would be a little too much."

"No," he persisted, "this is my affair. Girard, you know my money is with the notary. There is plenty. Raoul has not enough, perhaps not any. But he shall want nothing—you understand—nothing! It is my affair, all that he needs—but you shall not tell him—no! That is all."

Prosper had his way. But he did not see Vaillantcœur after he was carried home and put to bed in his cabin. Even if he had tried to do so, it would have been impossible. He could not see anybody. One of his eyes was entirely destroyed. The inflammation spread to the other, and all through the autumn he lay in his house, drifting along the edge of blindness, while Raoul lay in his house slowly getting well.

The curé went from one house to the other, but he did not carry any messages between them. If any were sent one way they were not received. And the other way, none were sent. Raoul did not speak of Prosper; and if one mentioned his name, Raoul shut his mouth and made no answer.

To the curé, of course, it was a distress and a misery.

To have a hatred like this unhealed, was a blot on the parish; it was a shame, as well as a sin. At last—it was already winter, the day before Christmas—the curé made up his mind that he would put forth one more great effort.

"Look you, my son," he said to Prosper, "I am going this afternoon to Raoul Vaillantcœur to make the reconciliation. You shall give me a word to carry to him. He shall hear it this time, I promise you. Shall I tell him what you have done for him, how you have cared for him?"

"No, never," said Prosper; "you shall not take that word from me. It is nothing. It will make worse trouble. I will never send it."

"What then?" said the priest. "Shall I tell him that you forgive him?"

"No, not that," answered Prosper, "that would be a foolish word. What would that mean? It is not I who can forgive. I was the one who struck hardest. It was he that fell from the tower."

"Well, then, choose the word for yourself. What shall it be? Come, I promise you that he shall hear it. I will take with me the notary, and the good man Girard, and the little Marie Antoinette. You shall hear an answer. What message?"

"Mon père," said Prosper, slowly, you shall tell him just this. I, Prosper Leclère, ask Raoul Vaillantcœur that he will forgive me for not fighting with him on the ground when he demanded it."

Yes, the message was given in precisely those words. Marie Antoinette stood within the door, Bergeron and Girard at the foot of the bed, and the curé spoke very clearly and firmly. Vaillantcœur rolled on his pillow and turned his face away. Then he sat up in bed, grunting a little with the pain in his shoulder, which was badly set. His black eyes snapped like the eyes of a wolverine in a corner.

"Forgive?" he said, "no, never. He is a coward. I will never forgive!"

A little later in the afternoon, when the rose of sunset

lay on the snowy hills, some one knocked at the door of Leclère's house.

"*Entrez!*" he cried. "Who is there? I see not very well by this light. Who is it?"

"It is me," said 'Toinette, her cheeks rosier than the snow outside, "nobody but me. I have come to ask you to tell me the rest about that new carriage—do you remember?"

III

The voice in the canoe behind me ceased. The rain let up. The *slish, slish* of the paddle stopped. The canoe swung sideways to the breeze. I heard the *rap, rap, rap* of a pipe on the gunwale, and the quick scratch of a match on the under side of the thwart.

"What are you doing, Ferdinand?"

"I go to light the pipe, m'sieu'."

"Is the story finished?"

"But yes—but no—I know not, m'sieu'. As you will."

"But what did old Girard say when his daughter broke her engagement and married a man whose eyes were spoiled?"

"He said that Leclère could see well enough to work with him in the store."

"And what did Vaillantcœur say when he lost his girl?"

"He said it was a cursed shame that one could not fight a blind man."

"And what did 'Toinette say?"

"She said she had chosen the bravest heart in Abbéville."

"And Prosper—what did he say?"

"M'sieu', I know not. He said it only to 'Toinette."

A Friend of Justice

A Friend of Justice

It was the black patch over his left eye that made all the trouble. In reality he was of a disposition most peaceful and propitiating, a friend of justice and fair dealing, strongly inclined to a domestic life, and capable of extreme devotion. He had a vivid sense of righteousness, it is true, and any violation of it was apt to heat his indignation to the boiling-point. When this occurred he was strong in the back, stiff in the neck, and fearless of consequences. But he was always open to friendly overtures and ready to make peace with honour.

Singularly responsive to every touch of kindness, desirous of affection, secretly hungry for caresses, he had a heart framed for love and tranquillity. But nature saw fit to put a black patch over his left eye; wherefore his days were passed in the midst of conflict and he lived the strenuous life.

How this sinister mark came to him, he never knew. Indeed it is not likely that he had any idea of the part that it played in his career. The attitude that the world took toward him from the beginning, an attitude of aggressive mistrust,—the rôle that he was expected and practically forced to assume in the drama of existence, the rôle of a hero of interminable strife,—must have seemed to him altogether mysterious and somewhat absurd. But his part was fixed by the black patch. It gave him an aspect so truculent and forbidding that all the elements of warfare gathered around him as hornets around a sugar barrel, and his appearance in public was like the raising of a flag for battle.

"You see that Pichou," said MacIntosh, the Hudson's Bay agent at Mingan, "you see yon big black-eye deevil? The savages call him Pichou because he's ugly as a lynx

129

—'*laid comme un pichou.*' Best sledge-dog and the gurliest
tyke on the North Shore. Only two years old and he can
lead a team already. But, man, he's just daft for the
fighting. Fought his mother when he was a pup and lamed
her for life. Fought two of his brothers and nigh killed
'em both. Every dog in the place has a grudge at him,
and hell's loose as oft as he takes a walk. I'm loath to part
with him, but I'll be selling him gladly for fifty dollars to
any man that wants a good sledge-dog, eh?—and a bit
collie-shangie every week."

Pichou had heard his name, and came trotting up to
the corner of the store where MacIntosh was talking with
old Grant the chief factor, who was on a tour of inspection along the North Shore, and Dan Scott, the agent
from Seven Islands, who had brought the chief down in
his chaloupe. Pichou did not understand what his master
had been saying about him: but he thought he was called,
and he had a sense of duty; and besides, he was wishful
to show proper courtesy to well-dressed and respectable
strangers. He was a great dog, thirty inches high at the
shoulder; broad-chested, with straight, sinewy legs; and
covered with thick, wavy, cream-coloured hair from the
tips of his short ears to the end of his busy tail—all except
the left side of his face. That was black from ear to nose
—coal-black; and in the centre of this storm-cloud his eye
gleamed like fire.

What did Pichou know about that ominous sign? No
one had ever told him. He had no looking-glass. He ran up
to the porch where the men were sitting, as innocent as a
Sunday-school scholar coming to the superintendent's
desk to receive a prize. But when old Grant, who had
grown pursy and nervous from long living on the fat of
the land at Ottawa, saw the black patch and the gleaming eye, he anticipated evil; so he hitched one foot up on
the porch, crying "Get out!" and with the other foot he
planted a kick on the side of the dog's head.

Pichou's nerve-centres had not been shaken by high
living. They acted with absolute precision and without
a tremor. His sense of justice was automatic, and his

teeth were fixed through the leg of the chief factor's boot, just below the calf.

For two minutes there was a small chaos in the post of the Honourable Hudson's Bay Company at Mingan. Grant howled bloody murder; MacIntosh swore in three languages and yelled for his dog-whip; three Indians and two French-Canadians wielded sticks and fence-pickets. But order did not arrive until Dan Scott knocked the burning embers from his big pipe on the end of the dog's nose. Pichou gasped, let go his grip, shook his head, and loped back to his quarters behind the barn, bruised, blistered, and intolerably perplexed by the mystery of life.

As he lay on the sand, licking his wounds, he remembered many strange things. First of all, there was the trouble with his mother.

She was a Labrador Husky, dirty yellowish gray, with bristling neck, sharp fangs, and green eyes, like a wolf. Her name was Babette. She had a fiendish temper, but no courage. His father was supposed to be a huge black and white Newfoundland that came over in a schooner from Miquelon. Perhaps it was from him that the black patch was inherited. And perhaps there were other things in the inheritance, too, which came from this nobler strain of blood: Pichou's unwillingness to howl with the other dogs when they made night hideous; his silent, dignified ways; his sense of fair play; his love of the water; his longing for human society and friendship.

But all this was beyond Pichou's horizon, though it was within his nature. He remembered only that Babette had taken a hate for him, almost from the first, and had always treated him worse than his all-yellow brothers. She would have starved him if she could. Once when he was half grown, she fell upon him for some small offence and tried to throttle him. The rest of the pack looked on snarling and slavering. He caught Babette by the foreleg and broke the bone. She hobbled away, shrieking. What else could he do? Must a dog let himself be killed by his mother?

As for his brothers—was it fair that two of them should fall foul of him about the rabbit which he had tracked and caught and killed? He would have shared it with them, if they had asked him, for they ran behind him on the trail. But when they both set their teeth in his neck, there was nothing to do but to lay them both out: which he did. Afterward he was willing enough to make friends, but they bristled and cursed whenever he came near them.

It was the same with everybody. If he went out for a walk on the beach, Vigneau's dogs or Simard's dogs regarded it as an insult, and there was a fight. Men picked up sticks, or showed him the butt-end of their dog-whips, when he made friendly approaches. With the children it was different; they seemed to like him a little; but never did he follow one of them that a mother did not call from the house-door: "Pierre! Marie! come away quick! That bad dog will bite you!" Once when he ran down to the shore to watch the boat coming in from the mail-steamer, the purser had refused to let the boat go to land, and called out, "M'sieu' MacIntosh, you git no malle dis trip, eef you not call avay dat dam' dog."

True, the Minganites seemed to take a certain kind of pride in his reputation. They had brought Chouart's big brown dog, Gripette, down from the Sheldrake to meet him; and after the meeting was over and Gripette had been revived with a bucket of water, everybody, except Chouart, appeared to be in good humour. The purser of the steamer had gone to the trouble of introducing a famous *boule-dogge* from Quebec, on the trip after that on which he had given such a hostile opinion of Pichou. The bulldog's intentions were unmistakable; he expressed them the moment he touched the beach; and when they carried him back to the boat on a fish-barrow many flattering words were spoken about Pichou. He was not insensible to them. But these tributes to his prowess were not what he really wanted. His secret desire was for tokens of affection. His position was honourable, but it was intolerably lonely and full of trouble. He sought peace and he found fights.

While he meditated dimly on these things, patiently trying to get the ashes of Dan Scott's pipe out of his nose, his heart was cast down and his spirit was disquieted within him. Was ever a decent dog so mishandled before? Kicked for nothing by a fat stranger, and then beaten by his own master!

In the dining-room of the Post, Grant was slowly and reluctantly allowing himself to be convinced that his injuries were not fatal. During this process considerable Scotch whiskey was consumed and there was much conversation about the viciousness of dogs. Grant insisted that Pichou was mad and had a devil. MacIntosh admitted the devil, but firmly denied the madness. The question was, whether the dog should be killed or not; and over this point there was like to be more bloodshed, until Dan Scott made his contribution to the argument: "If you shoot him, how can you tell whether he is mad or not? I'll give thirty dollars for him and take him home."

"If you do," said Grant, "you'll sail alone, and I'll wait for the steamer. Never a step will I go in the boat with the crazy brute that bit me."

"Suit yourself," said Dan Scott. "You kicked before he bit."

At daybreak he whistled the dog down to the chaloupe, hoisted sail, and bore away for Seven Islands. There was a secret bond of sympathy between the two companions on that hundred-mile voyage in an open boat. Neither of them realized what it was, but still it was there.

Dan Scott knew what it meant to stand alone, to face a small hostile world, to have a surfeit of fighting. The station of Seven Islands was the hardest in all the district of the ancient *Postes du Roi*. The Indians were surly and crafty. They knew all the tricks of the fur-trade. They killed out of season, and understood how to make a rusty pelt look black. The former agent had accommodated himself to his customers. He had no objection to shutting one of his eyes, so long as the other could see a chance of doing a stroke of business for himself. He also had a convenient weakness in the sense of smell, when there was an old stock of pork to work off on the savages. But all of Dan Scott's senses were strong, especially his sense of justice, and he came into the Post resolved to play a straight game with both hands, toward the Indians and toward the Honourable H. B. Company. The immediate results were reproofs from Ottawa and revilings from Seven Islands. Furthermore the free traders were against him because he objected to their selling rum to the savages.

It must be confessed that Dan Scott had a way with him that looked pugnacious. He was quick in his motions and carried his shoulders well thrown back. His voice was heavy. He used short words and few of them. His eyebrows were thick and they met over his nose. Then there was a broad white scar at one corner of his mouth. His appearance was not prepossessing, but at heart he was a philanthropist and a sentimentalist. He thirsted for gratitude and affection on a just basis. He had studied for eighteen months in the medical school at Montreal, and his chief delight was to practise gratuitously among the sick and wounded of the neighbourhood. His ambition for Seven Islands was to make it a northern suburb of Paradise, and for himself to become a full-fledged physician. Up to this time it seemed as if he would have to break more bones than he could set; and the closest connection of Seven Islands appeared to be with Purgatory.

First, there had been a question of suzerainty between Dan Scott and the local representative of the Astor family, a big half-breed descendant of a fur-trader, who was the virtual chief of the Indians hunting on the Ste. Marguérite: settled by knock-down arguments. Then there was a controversy with Napoleon Bouchard about the right to put a fish-house on a certain part of the beach: settled with a stick, after Napoleon had drawn a knife. Then there was a running warfare with Virgile and Ovide Boulianne, the free traders, who were his rivals in dealing with the Indians for their peltry: still unsettled. After this fashion the record of his relations with his fellow-citizens at Seven Islands was made up. He had their respect, but not their affection. He was the only Protestant, the only English-speaker, the most intelligent man, as well as the hardest hitter in the place, and he was very lonely. Perhaps it was this that made him take a fancy to Pichou. Their positions in the world were not unlike. He was not the first man who has wanted sympathy and found it in a dog.

Alone together, in the same boat, they made friends with each other easily. At first the remembrance of the hot pipe left a little suspicion in Pichou's mind; but this was removed by a handsome apology in the shape of a chunk of bread and a slice of meat from Dan Scott's lunch. After this they got on together finely. It was the first time in his life that Pichou had ever spent twenty-four hours away from other dogs; it was also the first time he had ever been treated like a gentleman. All that was best in him responded to the treatment. He could not have been more quiet and steady in the boat if he had been brought up to a seafaring life. When Dan Scott called him and patted him in the head, the dog looked up in the man's face as if he had found his God. And the man, looking down into the eye that was not disfigured by the black patch, saw something that he had been seeking for a long time.

All day the wind was fair and strong from the southeast. The chaloupe ran swiftly along the coast: past the broad mouth of the River Saint-Jean, with its cluster of white cottages: past the hill-encircled bay of the River Magpie, with its big fish-houses: past the fire-swept cliffs of Rivière-au-Tonnerre, and the turbulent, rocky shores of the Sheldrake: past the silver cascade of the Rivière-aux-Graines, and the mist of the hidden fall of the Rivière Manitou: past the long, desolate ridges of Cap Cormorant, where, at sunset, the wind began to droop away, and the tide was contrary. So the chaloupe felt its way cautiously toward the corner of the coast where the little Rivière-à-la-Truite comes tumbling in among the brown rocks, and found a haven for the night in the mouth of the river.

There was only one human dwelling-place in sight. As far as the eye could sweep, range after range of uninhabitable hills covered with the skeletons of dead forests; ledge after ledge of ice-worn granite thrust out like fangs into the foaming waves of the gulf. Nature, with

her teeth bare and her lips scarred: this was the landscape. And in the midst of it, on a low hill above the murmuring river, surrounded by the blanched trunks of fallen
trees, and the blackened débris of wood and moss, a
small, square, weather-beaten palisade of rough-hewn
spruce, and a patch of the bright green leaves and white
flowers of the dwarf cornel lavishing their beauty on a
lonely grave. This was the only habitation in sight—the
last home of the Englishman, Jack Chisholm, whose
story has yet to be told.

In the shelter of this hill Dan Scott cooked his supper
and shared it with Pichou. When night was dark he rolled
himself in his blanket, and slept in the stern of the boat,
with the dog at his side. Their friendship was sealed.

The next morning the weather was squally and full of
sudden anger. They crept out with difficulty through the
long rollers that barred the tiny harbour, and beat their
way along the coast. At Moisie they must run far out into
the gulf to avoid the treacherous shoals, and to pass
beyond the furious race of white-capped billows that
poured from the great river for miles into the sea. Then
they turned and made for the group of half-submerged
mountains and scattered rocks that Nature, in some freak
of fury, had thrown into the throat of Seven Islands Bay.
That was a difficult passage. The black shores were swept
by headlong tides. Tusks of granite tore the waves.
Baffled and perplexed, the wind flapped and whirled among
the cliffs. Through all this the little boat buffeted bravely
on till she reached the point of the Gran' Boule. Then a
strange thing happened.

The water was lumpy; the evening was growing thick;
a swirl of the tide and a shift of the wind caught the
chaloupe and swung her suddenly around. The mainsail
jibed, and before he knew how it happened Dan Scott was
overboard. He could swim but clumsily. The water
blinded him, choked him, dragged him down. Then he
felt Pichou gripping him by the shoulder, buoying him
up, swimming mightily toward the chaloupe which hung
trembling in the wind a few yards away. At last they
reached it and the man climbed over the stern and pulled

the dog after him. Dan Scott lay in the bottom of the boat, shivering, dazed, until he felt the dog's cold nose and warm breath against his cheek. He flung his arm around Pichou's neck.

"They said you were mad! God, if more men were mad like you!"

II

Pichou's work at Seven Islands was cut out for him on a generous scale. It is true that at first he had no regular canine labour to perform, for it was summer. Seven months of the year, on the North Shore, a sledge-dog's occupation is gone. He is the idlest creature in the universe.

But Pichou, being a new-comer, had to win his footing in the community; and that was no light task. With the humans it was comparatively easy. At the outset they mistrusted him on account of his looks. Virgile Boulianne asked: "Why did you buy such an ugly dog?" Ovide, who was the wit of the family, said: "I suppose M'sieu' Scott got a present for taking him."

"It's a good dog," said Dan Scott. "Treat him well and he'll treat you well. Kick him and I kick you."

Then he told what had happened off the point of Gran' Boule. The village decided to accept Pichou at his master's valuation. Moderate friendliness, with precautions, was shown toward him by everybody, except Napoleon Bouchard, whose distrust was permanent and took the form of a stick. He was a fat, fussy man; fat people seemed to have no affinity for Pichou.

But while the relations with the humans of Seven Islands were soon established on a fair footing, with the canines Pichou had a very different affair. They were not willing to accept any recommendations as to character. They judged for themselves; and they judged by appearances; and their judgment was utterly hostile to Pichou.

They decided that he was a proud dog, a fierce dog, a

bad dog, a fighter. He must do one of two things: stay at home in the yard of the Honourable H. B. Company, which is a thing that no self-respecting dog would do in the summer-time, when cod-fish heads are strewn along the beach; or fight his way from one end of the village to the other, which Pichou promptly did, leaving enemies behind every fence. Huskies never forget a grudge. They are malignant to the core. Hatred is the wine of cowardly hearts. This is as true of dogs as it is of men.

Then Pichou, having settled his foreign relations, turned his attention to matters at home. There were four other dogs in Dan Scott's team. They did not want Pichou for a leader, and he knew it. They were bitter with jealousy. The black patch was loathsome to them. They treated him disrespectfully, insultingly, grossly. Affairs came to a head when Pécan, a rusty gray dog who had great ambitions and little sense, disputed Pichou's tenure of a certain hambone. Dan Scott looked on placidly while the dispute was terminated. Then he washed the blood and sand from the gashes on Pécan's shoulder, and patted Pichou on the head.

"Good dog," he said. "You're the boss."

There was no further question about Pichou's leadership of the team. But the obedience of his followers was unwilling and sullen. There was no love in it. Imagine an English captain, with a Boer company, campaigning in the Ashantee country, and you will have a fair idea of Pichou's position at Seven Islands.

He did not shrink from its responsibilities. There were certain reforms in the community which seemed to him of vital importance, and he put them through.

First of all, he made up his mind that there ought to be peace and order on the village street. In the yards of the houses that were strung along it there should be home rule, and every dog should deal with trespassers as he saw fit. Also on the beach, and around the fish-shanties, and under the racks where the cod were drying, the right of the strong jaw should prevail, and differences of opinion should be adjusted in the old-fashioned way. But on the sandy road, bordered with a broken board-walk, which ran between the houses and the beach, courtesy and propriety must be observed. Visitors walked there. Children played there. It was the general promenade. It must be kept peaceful and decent. This was the First Law of the Dogs of Seven Islands: If two dogs quarrel on the street they must go elsewhere to settle it. It was highly unpopular, but Pichou enforced it with his teeth.

The Second Law was equally unpopular: No stealing from the Honourable H. B. Company. If a man bought bacon or corned-beef or any other delicacy, and stored it in an insecure place, or if he left fish on the beach over night, his dogs might act according to their inclination. Though Pichou did not understand how honest dogs could steal from their own master, he was willing to admit that this was their affair. His affair was that nobody should steal anything from the Post. It cost him many night watches, and some large battles to carry it out, but he did it. In the course of time it came to pass that the other dogs kept away from the Post altogether, to avoid temptations; and his own team spent most of their free time wandering about to escape discipline.

The Third Law was this: Strange dogs must be decently treated as long as they behave decently. This was contrary to all tradition, but Pichou insisted upon it. If a strange dog wanted to fight he should be accommodated with an antagonist of his own size. If he did not want to fight he should be politely smelled and allowed to pass through.

This Law originated on a day when a miserable, long-legged, black cur, a cross between a greyhound and a water-spaniel, strayed into Seven Islands from heaven knows where—weary, desolate, and bedraggled. All the dogs in the place attacked the homeless beggar. There was a howling fracas on the beach; and when Pichou arrived, the trembling cur was standing up to the neck in the water, facing a semicircle of snarling, snapping bullies who dared not venture out any farther. Pichou had no fear of the water. He swam out to the stranger, paid the smelling salute as well as possible under the circumstances, encouraged the poor creature to come ashore, warned off the other dogs, and trotted by the wanderer's side for miles down the beach until they disappeared around the point. What reward Pichou got for this polite escort, I do not know. But I saw him do the gallant deed; and I suppose this was the origin of the well-known and much-resisted Law of Strangers' Rights in Seven Islands.

The most recalcitrant subjects with whom Pichou had to deal in all these matters were the team of Ovide Boulianne. There were five of them, and up to this time they had been the best team in the village. They had one virtue: under the whip they could whirl a sledge over the snow farther and faster than a horse could trot in a day. But they had innumerable vices. Their leader, Carcajou, had a fleece like a merino ram. But under this coat of innocence he carried a heart so black that he would bite while he was wagging his tail. This smooth devil, and his four followers like unto himself, had sworn relentless hatred to Pichou, and they made his life difficult.

But his great and sufficient consolation for all toils and troubles was the friendship with his master. In the long summer evenings, when Dan Scott was making up his accounts in the store, or studying his pocket cyclopædia of medicine in the living-room of the Post, with its low beams and mysterious green-painted cupboards, Pichou would lie contentedly at his feet. In the frosty autumnal mornings, when the brant were flocking in the marshes at the head of the bay, they would go out hunting together in a skiff. And who could lie so still as Pichou when the game was approaching? Or who could spring so quickly and joyously to retrieve a wounded bird? But best of all were the long walks on Sunday afternoons, on the yellow beach that stretched away toward the Moisie, or through the fir-forest behind the Pointe des Chasseurs. Then master and dog had fellowship together in silence. To the dumb companion it was like walking with his God in the garden in the cool of the day.

When winter came, and snow fell, and waters froze, Pichou's serious duties began. The long, slim *cométique*, with its curving prow, and its runners of whalebone, was put in order. The harness of caribou-hide was repaired and strengthened. The dogs, even the most vicious of them, rejoiced at the prospect of doing the one thing that they could do best. Each one strained at his trace as if he would drag the sledge alone. Then the long tandem was straightened out, Dan Scott took his place on the low seat, cracked his whip, shouted *"Pouïtte! Pouïtte!"* and the equipage darted along the snowy track like a fifty-foot arrow.

Pichou was in the lead, and he showed his metal from the start. No need of the terrible *fouet* to lash him forward or to guide his course. A word was enough. "Hoc! Hoc! Hoc!" and he swung to the right, avoiding an airhole. "Re-re! Re-re!" and he veered to the left, dodging a heap of broken ice. Past the mouth of the Ste. Marguérite, twelve miles; past Les Jambons, twelve miles more; past the River of Rocks and La Pentecôte, fifteen miles more; into the little hamlet of Dean Men's Point, behind the Isle of the Wise Virgin, whither the amateur doctor had been summoned by telegraph to attend a patient with a broken arm—forty-three miles for the first day's run! Not bad. Then the dogs got their food for the day, one dried fish apiece; and at noon the next day, reckless of bleeding feet, they flew back over the same track, and broke their fast at Seven Islands before eight o'clock. The ration was the same, a single fish; always the same, except when it was varied by a cube of ancient, evil-smelling, potent whale's flesh, which a dog can swallow at a single gulp. Yet the dogs of the North Shore are never so full of vigour, courage, and joy of life as when the sledges are running. It is in summer, when food is plenty and work slack, that they sicken and die.

Pichou's leadership of his team became famous. Under his discipline the other dogs developed speed and steadiness. One day they made the distance to the Godbout in a single journey, a wonderful run of over eighty miles. But they loved their leader no better, though they followed him faster. And as for the other teams, especially Carcajou's, they were still firm in their deadly hatred for the dog with the black patch.

III

It was in the second winter after Pichou's coming to Seven Islands that the great trial of his courage arrived. Late in February an Indian runner on snowshoes staggered into the village. He brought news from the hunting-parties that were wintering far up on the Ste. Marguérite —good news and bad. First, they had already made a good hunting: for the *pelletrie*, that is to say. They had killed many otter, some fisher and beaver, and four silver foxes —a marvel of fortune. But then, for the food, the chase was bad, very bad—no caribou, no hare, no ptarmigan, nothing for many days. Provisions were very low. There were six families together. Then *la grippe* had taken hold of them. They were sick, starving. They would probably die, at least most of the women and children. It was a bad job.

Dan Scott had peculiar ideas of his duty toward the savages. He was not romantic, but he liked to do the square thing. Besides, he had been reading up on *la grippe,* and he had some new medicine for it, capsules from Montreal, very powerful—quinine, phenacetine, and morphine. He was as eager to try this new medicine as a boy is to fire off a new gun. He loaded the *cométique* with provisions and the medicine-chest with capsules, harnessed his team, and started up the river. Thermometer thirty degrees below zero; air like crystal; snow six feet deep on the level.

The first day's journey was slow, for the going was soft, and the track, at places, had to be broken out with snow-shoes. Camp was made at the foot of the big fall— a hole in snow, a bed of boughs, a hot fire and a blanket stretched on a couple of sticks to reflect the heat, the dogs on the other side of the fire, and Pichou close to his master.

In the morning there was the steep hill beside the fall to climb; alternately soft and slippery, now a slope of glass and now a treacherous drift of yielding feathers; it was a road set on end. But Pichou flattened his back and strained his loins and dug his toes into the snow and would not give back an inch. When the rest of the team balked the long whip slashed across their backs and recalled them to their duty. At last their leader topped the ridge, and the others struggled after him. Before them stretched the great dead-water of the river, a straight white path to No-man's-land. The snow was smooth and level, and the crust was hard enough to bear. Pichou settled down to his work at a glorious pace. He seemed to know that he must do his best, and that something important depended on the quickness of his legs. On through the glittering solitude, on through the death-like silence, sped the *cométique*, between the interminable walls of the forest, past the mouths of nameless rivers, under the shadow of grim mountains. At noon Dan Scott boiled the kettle, and ate his bread and bacon. But there was nothing for the dogs, not even for Pichou; for discipline is discipline, and the best of sledge-dogs will not run well after he has been fed.

Then forward again, along the lifeless road; slowly over rapids, where the ice was rough and broken; swiftly over still waters, where the way was level; until they came to the foot of the last lake, and camped for the night. The Indians were but a few miles away, at the head of the lake, and it would be easy to reach them in the morning.

But there was another camp on the Ste. Marguérite that night, and it was nearer to Dan Scott than the Indians were. Ovide Boulianne had followed him up the river, close on his track, which made the going easier.

"Does that *sacré bourgeois* suppose that I allow him all that *pelletrie* to himself and the *Compagnie?* Four silver fox, besides otter and beaver? *Non, merci!* I take some provision, and some whiskey. I go to make trade also." Thus spoke the shrewd Ovide, proving that commerce is no less daring, no less resolute, than philanthropy. The only difference is in the motive, and that is not always visible. Ovide camped the second night at a bend of the river, a mile below the foot of the lake. Between him and Dan Scott there was a hill covered with a dense thicket of spruce.

By what magic did Carcajou know that Pichou, his old enemy, was so near him in that vast wilderness of white death? By what mysterious language did he communicate his knowledge to his companions and stir the sleeping hatred in their hearts and mature the conspiracy of revenge?

Pichou, sleeping by the fire, was awakened by the fall of a lump of snow from the branch of a shaken evergreen. That was nothing. But there were other sounds in the forest, faint, stealthy, inaudible to an ear less keen than his. He crept out of the shelter and looked into the wood. He could see shadowy forms, stealing among the trees, gliding down the hill. Five of them. Wolves, doubtless! He must guard the provisions. By this time the rest of his team were awake. Their eyes glittered. They stirred uneasily. But they did not move from the dying fire. It was no concern of theirs what their leader chose to do out of hours. In the traces they would follow him, but there was no loyalty in their hearts. Pichou stood alone by the sledge, waiting for the wolves.

But these were no wolves. They were assassins. Like a company of soldiers, they lined up together and rushed silently down the slope. Like lightning they leaped upon the solitary dog and struck him down. In an instant, before Dan Scott could throw off his blanket and seize the loaded butt of his whip, Pichou's throat and breast were torn to rags, his life-blood poured upon the snow, and his murderers were slinking away, slavering and muttering through the forest.

Dan Scott knelt beside his best friend. At a glance he saw that the injury was fatal. "Well done, Pichou!" he murmured, "you fought a good fight."

And the dog, by a brave effort, lifted the head with the black patch on it, for the last time, licked his master's hand, and then dropped back upon the snow—contented, happy, dead.

There is but one drawback to a dog's friendship. It does not last long enough.

End of the story? Well, if you care for the other people in it, you shall hear what became of them. Dan Scott went on to the head of the lake and found the Indians, and fed them and gave them his medicine, and all of them got well except two, and they continued to hunt along the Ste. Marguérite every winter and trade with the Honourable H. B. Company. Not with Dan Scott, however, for before that year was ended he resigned his post, and went to Montreal to finish his course in medicine; and now he is a respected physician in Ontario. Married; three children; useful; prosperous. But before he left Seven Islands he went up the Ste. Marguérite in the summer, by canoe, and made a grave for Pichou's bones, under a blossoming ash tree, among the ferns and wild flowers.

The White Blot

The White Blot

I

The real location of a city house depends upon the pictures which hang upon its walls. They are its neighbourhood and its outlook. They confer upon it that touch of life and character, that power to beget love and bind friendship, which a country house receives from its surrounding landscape, the garden that embraces it, the stream that runs near it, and the shaded paths that lead to and from its door.

By this magic of pictures my narrow, upright slice of living-space in one of the brown-stone strata on the eastward slope of Manhattan Island is transferred to an open and agreeable site. It has windows that look toward the woods and the sunset, watergates by which a little boat is always waiting, and secret passageways leading into fair places that are frequented by persons of distinction and charm. No darkness of night obscures these outlets; no neighbour's house shuts off the view; no drifted snow of winter makes them impassable. They are always free, and through them I go out and in upon my adventures.

One of these picture-wanderings has always appeared to me so singular that I would like, if it were possible, to put it into words.

It was Pierrepont who first introduced me to the picture —Pierrepont the good-natured: of whom one of his friends said that he was like Mahomet's Bridge of Paradise, because he was so hard to cross: to which another added that there was also a resemblance in the fact that he led to a region of beautiful illusions which he never entered. He is one of those enthusiastic souls who are always discovering a new writer, a new painter, a new view from

some old wharf by the river, a new place to obtain pic-
turesque dinners at a grotesque price. He swung out of
his office, with his long-legged, easy stride, and nearly
ran me down, as I was plodding up-town through the
languor of a late spring afternoon, on one of those duty-
walks which conscience offers as a sacrifice to digestion.

"Why, what is the matter with you?" he cried, as he
linked his arm through mine, "you look outdone, tired all
the way through to your backbone. Have you been reading
the 'Anatomy of Melancholy,' or something by one of the
new British female novelists? You will have *la grippe* in
your mind if you don't look out. But I know what you need.
Come with me, and I will do you good."

So saying, he drew me out of clanging Broadway into
one of the side streets that run toward the placid region
of Washington Square. "No, no," I answered, feeling,
even in the act of resistance, the pleasure of his cheerful
guidance, "you are altogether wrong. I don't need a dinner at your new-found Bulgarian *table-d'hôte*—seven
courses for seventy-five cents, and the wine thrown out;
nor some of those wonderful Mexican cheroots warranted
to eradicate the tobacco-habit; nor a draught of your
South American melon sherbet that cures all pains, except those which it causes. None of these things will help
me. The doctor suggests that they do not suit my temper-
ament. Let us go home together and have a shower-bath
and a dinner of herbs, with just a reminiscence of the
stalled ox—and a bout at backgammon to wind up the evening. That will be the most comfortable prescription."

"But you mistake me," said he; "I am not thinking of
any creature comforts for you. I am prescribing for your
mind. There is a picture that I want you to see; not a
coloured photograph, nor an exercise in anatomical drawing; but a real picture that will rest the eyes of your
heart. Come away with me to Morgenstern's gallery, and
be healed."

As we turned into the lower end of Fifth Avenue, it
seemed as if I were being gently floated along between
the modest apartment-houses and old-fashioned dwellings, and prim, respectable churches, on the smooth cur-

rent of Pierrepont's talk about his new-found picture. How often a man has cause to return thanks for the enthusiasms of his friends! They are the little fountains that run down from the hills to refresh the mental desert of the despondent.

"You remember Falconer," continued Pierrepont, "Temple Falconer, that modest, quiet, proud fellow who came out of the South a couple of years ago and carried off the landscape prize at the Academy last year, and then disappeared? He had no intimate friends here, and no one knew what had become of him. But now this picture appears, to show what he has been doing. It is an evening scene, a revelation of the beauty of sadness, an idea expressed in colours—or rather, a real impression of Nature that awakens an ideal feeling in the heart. It does not define everything and say nothing, like so many paintings. It tells no story, but I know it fits into one. There is not a figure in it, and yet it is alive with sentiment; it suggests thoughts which cannot be put into words. Don't you love the pictures that have that power of suggestion —quiet and strong, like Homer Martin's 'Light-house' up at the Century, with its sheltered bay heaving softly under the pallid greenish sky of evening, and the calm, steadfast glow of the lantern brightening into readiness for all the perils of night and coming storm? How much more powerful that is than all the conventional pictures of light-houses on inaccessible cliffs, with white foam streaming from them like the ends of a schoolboy's comforter in a gale of wind! I tell you the real painters are the fellows who love pure nature because it is so human. They don't need to exaggerate, and they don't dare to be affected. They are not afraid of the reality, and they are not ashamed of the sentiment. They don't paint everything that they see, but they see everything that they paint. And this picture makes me sure that Falconer is one of them."

By this time we had arrived at the door of the house where Morgenstern lives and moves and makes his profits, and were admitted to the shrine of the Commercial Apollo and the Muses in Trade.

It has often seemed to me as if that little house were a silent epitome of modern art criticism, an automatic indicator, or perhaps regulator, of the æsthetic taste of New York. On the first floor, surrounded by all the newest fashions in antiquities and *bric-à-brac*, you will see the art of to-day—the works of painters who are precisely in the focus of advertisement, and whose names call out an instant round of applause in the auction-room. On the floors above, in degrees of obscurity deepening toward the attic, you will find the art of yesterday—the pictures which have passed out of the glare of popularity without yet arriving at the mellow radiance of old masters. In the basement, concealed in huge packing-cases, and marked "*Paris— Fragile*,"—you will find the art of to-morrow; the paintings of the men in regard to whose names, styles, and personal traits, the foreign correspondents and prophetic critics in the newspapers, are now diffusing in the public mind that twilight of familiarity and ignorance which precedes the sunrise of marketable fame.

The affable and sagacious Morgenstern was already well acquainted with the waywardness of Pierrepont's admiration, and with my own persistent disregard of current quotations in the valuation of works of art. He regarded us, I suppose, very much as Robin Hood would have looked upon a pair of plain yeomen who had strayed into his lair. The knights of capital, and coal barons, and rich merchants were his natural prey, but toward this poor but honest couple it would be worthy only of a Gentile robber to show anything but courteous and fair dealing.

He expressed no surprise when he heard what we wanted to see, but smiled tolerantly and led the way, not into the well-defined realm of the past, the present, or the future, but into a region of uncertain fortunes, a limbo of acknowledged but unrewarded merits, a large back room devoted to the works of American painters. Here we found Falconer's picture; and the dealer, with that instinctive tact which is the best part of his business capital, left us alone to look at it.

It showed the mouth of a little river: a secluded lagoon,

where the shallow tides rose and fell with vague lassitude, following the impulse of prevailing winds more than the strong attraction of the moon. But now the unsailed harbour was quite still, in the pause of the evening; and the smooth undulations were caressed by a hundred opalescent hues, growing deeper toward the west, where the river came in. Converging lines of trees stood dark against the sky; a cleft in the woods marked the course of the stream, above which the reluctant splendours of an autumnal day were dying in ashes of roses, while three tiny clouds, poised high in air, burned red with the last glimpse of the departed sun.

On the right was a reedy point running out into the bay, and behind it, on a slight rise of ground, an antique house with tall white pillars. It was but dimly outlined in the gathering shadows; yet one could imagine its stately, formal aspect, its precise garden with beds of old-fashioned flowers and straight paths bordered with box, and a little arbour overgrown with honeysuckle. I know not by what subtlety of delicate and indescribable touches—a slight inclination in one of the pillars, a broken line which might indicate an unhinged gate, a drooping resignation in the foliage of the yellowing trees, a tone of sadness in the blending of subdued colours—the painter had suggested that the place was deserted. But the truth was unmistakable. An air of loneliness and pensive sorrow breathed from the picture; a sigh of longing and regret. It was haunted by sad, sweet memories of some untold story of human life.

In the corner Falconer had put his signature, *T. F.,* "Larmone," 189–, and on the border of the picture he had faintly traced some words, which we made out at last—

> *A spirit haunts the year's last hours.*

Pierrepont took up the quotation and completed it—

> *A spirit haunts the year's last hours,*
> *Dwelling amid these yellowing bowers:*
> *To himself he talks;*
> *For at eventide, listening earnestly,*

At his work you may hear him sob and sigh,
 In the walks;
Earthward he boweth the heavy stalks
Of the mouldering flowers:
Heavily hangs the broad sunflower
  Over its grave i' the earth so chilly;
Heavily hangs the hollyhock,
  Heavily hangs the tiger-lily.

"That is very pretty poetry, gentlemen," said Morgenstern, who had come in behind us, "but is it not a little vague? You like it, but you cannot tell exactly what it means. I find the same fault in the picture from my point of view. There is nothing in it to make a paragraph about, no anecdote, no experiment in technique. It is impossible to persuade the public to admire a picture unless you can tell them precisely the points on which they must fix their admiration. And that is why, although the painting is a good one, I should be willing to sell it at a low price."

He named a sum of money in three figures, so small that Pierrepont, who often buys pictures by proxy, could not conceal his surprise.

"Certainly I should consider that a good bargain, simply for investment," said he. "Falconer's name alone ought to be worth more than that, ten years from now. He is a rising man."

"No, Mr. Pierrepont," replied the dealer, "the picture is worth what I ask for it, for I would not commit the impertinence of offering a present to you or your friend; but it is worth no more. Falconer's name will not increase in value. The catalogue of his works is too short for fame to take much notice of it; and this is the last. Did you not hear of his death last fall? I do not wonder, for it happened at some place down on Long Island—a name that I never saw before, and have forgotten now. There was not even an obituary in the newspapers."

"And besides," he continued, after a pause, "I must not conceal from you that the painting has a blemish. It is not always visible, since you have failed to detect it; but it is more noticeable in some lights than in others; and, do what I will, I cannot remove it. This alone would prevent the painting from being a good investment. Its market value will never rise."

He turned the canvas sideways to the light, and the defect became apparent.

It was a dim, oblong, white blot in the middle distance; a nebulous blur in the painting, as if there had been some chemical impurity in the pigment causing it to fade, or rather as if a long drop of some acid, or perhaps a splash of salt water, had fallen upon the canvas while it was wet, and bleached it. I knew little of the possible causes of such a blot, but enough to see that it could not be erased without painting over it, perhaps not even then. And yet it seemed rather to enhance than to weaken the attraction which the picture had for me.

"Your candour does you credit, Mr. Morgenstern," said I, "but you know me well enough to be sure that what you have said will hardly discourage me. For I have never been an admirer of 'cabinet finish' in works of art. Nor have I been in the habit of buying them, as a Circassian father trains his daughters, with an eye to the market. They come into my house for my own pleasure, and when the time arrives that I can see them no longer, it will not matter much to me what price they bring in the auction-room. This landscape pleases me so thoroughly that, if you will let us take it with us this evening, I will send you a check for the amount in the morning."

So we carried off the painting in a cab; and all the way home I was in the pleasant excitement of a man who is about to make an addition to his house; while Pierrepont was conscious of the glow of virtue which comes of having done a favour to a friend and justified your own critical judgment at one stroke.

After dinner we hung the painting over the chimney-piece in the room called the study (because it was consecrated to idleness), and sat there far into the night, talking of the few times we had met Falconer at the club, and of his reticent manner, which was broken by curious flashes of impersonal confidence when he spoke not of himself but of his art. From this we drifted into memories of good comrades who had walked beside us but a few days in the path of life, and then disappeared, yet left us feeling as if we cared more for them than for the men whom we see every day; and of young geniuses who had never reached the goal; and of many other glimpses of "the light that failed," until the lamp was low and it was time to say good-night.

II

For several months I continued to advance in intimacy with my picture. It grew more familiar, more suggestive; the truth and beauty of it came home to me constantly. Yet there was something in it not quite apprehended; a sense of strangeness; a reserve which I had not yet penetrated.

One night in August I found myself practically alone, so far as human intercourse was concerned, in the populous, weary city. A couple of hours of writing had produced nothing that would bear the test of sunlight, so I anticipated judgment by tearing up the spoiled sheets of paper, and threw myself upon the couch before the empty fireplace. It was a dense, sultry night, with electricity thickening the air, and a trouble of distant thunder rolling far away on the rim of the cloudy sky—one of those nights of restless dulness, when you wait and long for something to happen, and yet feel despondently that nothing ever will happen again. I passed through a region of aimless thoughts into one of migratory and unfinished dreams, and dropped from that into an empty gulf of sleep.

How late it was when I drifted back toward the shore of consciousness, I cannot tell. But the student-lamp on the table had burned out, and the light of the gibbous moon was creeping in through the open windows. Slowly the pale illumination crept up the eastern wall, like a tide rising as the moon declined. Now it reached the mantel-shelf and overflowed the bronze heads of Homer and the Indian Bacchus and the Egyptian image of Isis with the infant Horus. Now it touched the frame of the picture and lapped over the edge. Now it rose to the shadowy house and the dim garden, in the midst of which I saw the white blot more distinctly than ever before.

It seemed now to have taken a new shape, like the slender form of a woman, robed in flowing white. And as I watched it through half-closed eyes, the figure appeared to move and tremble and wave to and fro, as if it were a ghost.

A haunted picture! Why should it not be so? A haunted ruin, a haunted forest, a haunted ship,—all these have been seen, or imagined, and reported, and there are learned societies for investigating such things. Why should not a picture have a ghost in it?

My mind, in that curiously vivid state which lies between waking and sleeping, went through the form of careful reasoning over the question. If there may be some subtle connection between a house and the spirits of the people who have once lived in it,—and wise men have believed this,—why should there be any impassable gulf between a picture and the vanished lives out of which it has grown? All the human thought and feeling which have passed into it through the patient toil of art, remain forever embodied there. A picture is the most living and personal thing that a man can leave behind him. When we look at it we see what he saw, hour after hour, day after day, and we see it through his mood and impression, coloured by his emotion, tinged with his personality. Surely, if the spirits of the dead are not extinguished, but only veiled and hidden, and if it were possible by any means that their presence could flash for a moment through the veil, it would be most natural that they should come back again to hover around the work into which their experience and passion had been woven. Here, if anywhere, they would "Revisit the pale glimpses of the moon." Here, if anywhere, we might catch fleeting sight, as in a glass darkly, of the visions that passed before them while they worked.

This much of my train of reasoning along the edge of the dark, I remember sharply. But after this, all was confused and misty. The shore of consciousness receded. I floated out again on the ocean of forgotten dreams. When I woke, it was with a quick start, as if my ship had been made fast, silently and suddenly, at the wharf of reality, and the bell rang for me to step ashore.

But the vision of the white blot remained clear and distinct. And the question that it had brought to me, the chain of thoughts that had linked themselves to it, lingered through the morning, and made me feel sure that there was an untold secret in Falconer's life and that the clew to it must be sought in the history of his last picture.

But how to trace the connection? Every one who had known Falconer, however slightly, was out of town. There was no clew to follow. Even the name "Larmone" gave me no help; for I could not find it on any map of Long Island. It was probably the fanciful title of some old country-place, familiar only to the people who had lived there.

But the very remoteness of the problem, its lack of contact with the practical world, fascinated me. It was like something that had drifted away in the fog, on a sea of unknown and fluctuating currents. The only possible way to find it was to commit yourself to the same wandering tides and drift after it, trusting to a propitious fortune that you might be carried in the same direction; and after a long, blind, unhurrying chase, one day you might feel a faint touch, a jar, a thrill along the side of your boat, and, peering through the fog, lay your hand at last, without surprise, upon the very object of your quest.

III

As it happened, the means for such a quest were at my disposal. I was part owner of a boat which had been built for hunting and fishing cruises on the shallow waters of the Great South Bay. It was a deliberate, but not inconvenient, craft, well named the Patience; and my turn for using it had come. Zekiel, the captain, crew, and cook, was the very man that I would have chosen for such an expedition. He knew every shoal and channel of the tortuous waters. He asked nothing better than to set out on a voyage without a port; sailing aimlessly eastward day after day, through the long chain of landlocked bays, with the sea plunging behind the sand-dunes on our right, and the shores of Long Island sleeping on our left; anchoring every evening in some little cove or estuary, where Zekiel could sit on the cabin roof, smoking his corn-cob pipe, and meditating on the vanity and comfort of life, while I pushed off through the mellow dusk to explore every creek and bend of the shore, in my light canoe.

There was nothing to hasten our voyage. The three weeks' vacation was all but gone, when the Patience groped her way through a narrow, crooked channel in a wide salt-meadow, and entered the last of the series of bays. A few houses straggled down a point of land; the village of Quantock lay a little farther back. Beyond that was a belt of woods reaching to the water; and from these the south-country road emerged to cross the upper end of the bay on a low causeway with a narrow bridge of planks at the central point. Here was our Ultima Thule. Not even the Patience could thread the eye of this needle, or float through the shallow marsh-canal farther to the east.

We anchored just in front of the bridge, and as I pushed the canoe beneath it, after supper, I felt the indefinable sensation of having passed that way before. I knew beforehand what the little boat would drift into. The broad saffron light of evening fading over a still lagoon; two converging lines of pine trees running back into the sunset; a grassy point upon the right; and behind that a neglected garden, a tangled bower of honeysuckle, a straight path bordered with box, leading to a deserted house with a high, white-pillared porch—yes, it was Larmone.

In the morning I went up to the village to see if I could find trace of my artist's visit to the place. There was no difficulty in the search, for he had been there often. The people had plenty of recollections of him, but no real memory, for it seemed as if none of them had really known him.

"Queer kinder fellow," said a wrinkled old bayman with whom I walked up the sandy road; "I seen him a good deal round here, but 'twan't like havin' any 'quaintance with him. He allus kep' himself to himself, pooty much. Used ter stay round 'Squire Ladoo's place most o' the time—keepin' comp'ny with the gal I guess. Larmone? Yaas, that's what *they* called it, but we don't go much on fancy names down here. No, the painter did n' 'zactly live there, but it 'mounted to the same thing. Las' summer they was all away, house shet up, painter hangin' round all the time, 's if he looked fur 'em to come back any minnit. Purfessed to be paintin', but I don' see's he did much. Lived up to Mort Halsey's; died there too; year ago this fall. Guess Mis' Halsey can tell ye most of any one 'bout him."

At the boarding-house (with wide, low verandas, now forsaken by the summer boarders), which did duty for a village inn, I found Mrs. Halsey; a notable housewife, with a strong taste for ancestry, and an uncultivated world of romance still brightening her soft brown eyes. She knew all the threads in the story that I was following; and the interest with which she spoke made it evident that she had often woven them together in the winter evenings on patterns of her own.

Judge Ledoux had come to Quantock from the South during the war, and built a house there like the one he used to live in. There were three things he hated: slavery and war and society. But he always loved the South more than the North, and lived like a foreigner, polite enough, but very retired. His wife died after a few years, and left him alone with a little girl. Claire grew up as pretty as a picture, but very shy and delicate. About two years ago Mr. Falconer had come down from the city; he stayed at Larmone first, and then he came to the boarding-house, but he was over at the Ledoux' house almost all the time. He was a Southerner too, and a relative of the family; a real gentleman, and very proud though he was poor. It seemed strange that he should not live with them, but perhaps he felt more free over here. Every one thought he must be engaged to Clarie, but he was not the kind of a man that you could ask questions about himself. A year ago last winter he had gone up to the city and taken all his things with him. He had never stayed away so long before. In the spring the Ledoux had gone to Europe; Claire seemed to be falling into a decline; her sight seemed to be failing, and her father said she must see a famous doctor and have a change of air.

"Mr. Falconer came back in May," continued the good lady, "as if he expected to find them. But the house was shut up and nobody knew just where they were. He seemed to be all taken aback; it was queer if he didn't know about it, intimate as he had been; but he never said anything, and made no inquiries; just seemed to be waiting, as if there was nothing else for him to do. We would have told him in a minute, if we had anything to tell. But all we could do was to guess there must have been some kind of a quarrel between him and the Judge; and if there was, he must know best about it himself.

"All summer long he kept going over to the house and wandering around in the garden. In the fall he began to paint a picture, but it was very slow painting; he would go over in the afternoon and come back long after dark, damp with the dew and fog. He kept growing paler and weaker and more silent. Some days he did not speak more than a dozen words, but always kind and pleasant. He was just dwindling away; and when the picture was almost done a fever took hold of him. The doctor said it was malaria, but it seemed to me more like a trouble in the throat, a kind of dumb misery. And one night, in the third quarter of the moon, just after the tide turned to run out, he raised up in the bed and tried to speak, but he was gone.

"We tried to find out his relations, but there didn't seem to be any, except the Ledoux, and they were out of reach. So we sent the picture up to our cousin in Brooklyn, and it sold for about enough to pay Mr. Falconer's summer's board and the cost of his funeral. There was nothing else that he left of any value, except a few books;

perhaps you would like to look at them, if you were his friend?

"I never saw any one that I seemed to know so little and like so well. It was a disappointment in love, of course, and they all said that he died of a broken heart; but I think it was because his heart was too full, and wouldn't break.

"And oh!—I forgot to tell you; a week after he was gone there was a notice in the paper that Claire Ledoux had died suddenly, on the last of August, at some place in Switzerland. Her father is still away travelling. And so the whole story is broken off and will never be finished. Will you look at the books?"

Nothing is more pathetic, to my mind, than to take up the books of one who is dead. Here is his name, with perhaps a note of the place where the volume was bought or read, and the marks on the pages that he liked best. Here are the passages that gave him pleasure, and the thoughts that entered into his life and formed it; they became part of him, but where has he carried them now?

Falconer's little library was an unstudied choice, and gave a hint of his character. There was a New Testament in French, with his name written in a slender, woman's hand; three or four volumes of stores, Cable's "Old Creole Days," Allen's "Kentucky Cardinal," Page's "In Old Virginia," and the like; "Henry Esmond" and Amiel's "Journal" and Lamartine's "Raphael"; and a few volumes of poetry, among them one of Sidney Lanier's, and one of Tennyson's earlier poems.

There was also a little morocco-bound book of manuscript notes. This I begged permission to carry away with me, hoping to find in it something which would throw light upon my picture, perhaps even some message to be carried, some hint or suggestion of something which the writer would fain have had done for him, and which I promised myself faithfully to perform, as a test of an imagined friendship—imagined not in the future, but in the impossible past.

I read the book in this spirit, searching its pages carefully, through the long afternoon, in the solitary cabin

of my boat. There was nothing at first but an ordinary
diary; a record of the work and self-denials of a poor
student of art. Then came the date of his first visit to
Larmone, and an expression of the pleasure of being with
his own people again after a lonely life, and some chronicle
of his occupations there, studies for pictures, and idle
days that were summed up in a phrase: "On the bay," or
"In the woods."

After this the regular succession of dates was broken,
and there followed a few scraps of verse, irregular and
unfinished, bound together by the thread of a name—
"Claire among her Roses," "A Ride through the Pines
with Claire," "An Old Song of Claire's," "The Blue Flower
in Claire's Eyes." It was not poetry, but such an unconscious
tribute to the power and beauty of poetry as unfolds
itself almost inevitably from youthful love, as naturally as
the blossoms unfold from the apple trees in May. If you
pick them they are worthless. They charm only in their
own time and place.

A date told of his change from Larmone to the village,
and this was written below it: "Too heavy a sense of
obligation destroys freedom, and only a free man can
dare to love."

Then came a number of fragments indicating trouble
of mind and hesitation; the sensitiveness of the artist,
the delicate, self-tormenting scruples of the lonely idealist,
the morbid pride of the young poor man, contending
with an impetuous passion and forcing it to surrender, or
at least to compromise.

"What right has a man to demand everything and offer
nothing in return except an ambition and a hope? Love
must come as a giver, not as a beggar."

"A knight should not ask to wear his lady's colours
until he has won his spurs."

"King Cophetua and the beggar-maid—very fine! but
the other way—humiliating."

"A woman may take everything from a man, wealth
and fame and position. But there is only one thing
that a man may accept from a woman—something that
she alone can give—happiness."

"Self-respect is less than love, but it is the trellis that holds love up from the ground; break it down, and all the flowers are in the dust, the fruit is spoiled."

"And yet"—so the man's thought shone through everywhere—"I think she must know that I love her, and why I cannot speak."

One entry was written in a clearer, stronger hand: "An end of hesitation. The longest way is the shortest. I am going to the city to work for the Academy prize, to think of nothing else until I win it, and then come back with it to Claire, to tell her that I have a future, and that it is hers. If I spoke of it now it would be like claiming the reward before I had done the work. I have told her only that I am going to prove myself an artist, *and to live for what I love best.* She understood, I am sure, for she would not lift her eyes to me, but her hand trembled as she gave me the blue flower from her belt."

The date of his return to Larmone was marked, but the page was blank, as the day had been.

Some pages of dull self-reproach and questioning and bewildered regret followed.

"Is it possible that she has gone away, without a word, without a sign, after what has passed between us? It is not fair. Surely I had some claim."

"But what claim, after all? I asked for nothing. And was it not pride that kept me silent, taking it for granted that if I asked, she would give?"

"It was a mistake; she did not understand, nor care."

"It was my fault; I might at least have told her that I loved her, though she could not have answered me."

"It is too late now. To-night, while I was finishing the picture, I saw her in the garden. Her spirit, all in white, with a blue flower in her belt. I knew she was dead across the sea. I tried to call to her, but my voice made no sound. She seemed not to see me. She moved like one in a dream, straight on, and vanished. Is there no one who can tell her? Must she never know that I loved her?"

The last thing in the book was a printed scrap of paper that lay between the leaves:

IRREVOCABLE

Would the gods might give
Another field for human strife;
Man must live one life
Ere he learns to live.
Ah, friend, in thy deep grave,
What now can change; what now can save?

So there was a message after all, but it could never be carried; a task for a friend, but it was impossible. What better thing could I do with the poor little book than bury it in the garden in the shadow of Larmone? The story of a silent fault, hidden in silence. How many of life's deepest tragedies are only that: no great transgression, no shock of conflict, no sudden catastrophe with its answering thrill of courage and resistance: only a mistake made in the darkness, and under the guidance of what seemed a true and noble motive; a failure to see the right path at the right moment, and a long wandering beyond it; a word left unspoken until the ears that should have heard it are sealed, and the tongue that should have spoken it is dumb.

The soft sea-fog clothed the night with clinging darkness; the faded leaves hung slack and motionless from the trees, waiting for their fall; the tense notes of the surf beyond the sand-dunes vibrated through the damp air like chords from some mighty *violono*; large, warm drops wept from the arbour while I sat in the garden, holding the poor little book, and thinking of the white blot in the record of a life that was too proud to bend to the happiness that was meant for it.

There are men like that: not many perhaps, but a few; and they are the ones who suffer most keenly in this world of half-understanding and clouded knowledge. There is a pride, honourable and sensitive, that imperils the realization of love, puts it under a spell of silence and reserve, makes it sterile of blossoms and impotent of fruits. For what is it, after all, but a subtle, spiritual worship of self? And what was Falconer's resolve not to tell this girl that he loved her until he had won fame and position, but a secret, unconscious setting of himself above her? For surely, if love is supreme, it does not need to wait for anything else to lend it worth and dignity. The very sweetness and power of it lie in the confession of one life as dependent upon another for its fulfilment. It is made strong in its very weakness. It is the only thing, after all, that can break the prison bars and set the heart free from itself. The pride that hinders it, enslaves it. Love's first duty is to be true to itself, in word and deed. Then, having spoken truth and acted verity, it may call on honour to keep it pure and steadfast.

If Falconer had trusted Claire, and showed her his heart without reserve, would she not have understood him and helped him? It was the pride of independence, the passion of self-reliance that drew him away from her and divided his heart from hers in a dumb isolation. But Claire,—was not she also in fault? Might she not have known, should not she have taken for granted, the truth which must have been so easy to read in Falconer's face, though he never put it into words? And yet with her there was something very different from the pride that kept him silent. The virgin reserve of a young girl's heart is more sacred than any pride of self. It is the maiden instinct which makes the woman always the shrine, and never the pilgrim. She is not the seeker, but the one sought. She does not take anything for granted. She has the right to wait for the voice, the word, the avowal. Then, and not till then, if the pilgrim be the chosen one, the shrine may open to receive him.

Not all women believe this; but those who do are the ones best worth seeking and winning. And Claire was one of them. It seemed to me, as I mused, half dreaming, on the unfinished story of these two lives that had missed each other in the darkness, that I could see her figure moving through the garden, beyond where the pallid bloom of the tall cosmos-flower bent to the fitful breeze. Her robe was like the waving of the mist. Her face was fair, and very fair, for all its sadness: a blue flower, faint as a shadow on the snow, trembled at her waist, as she paced to and fro along the path.

I murmured to myself, "Yet he loved her: and she loved him. Can pride be stronger than love?"

Perhaps, after all, the lingering and belated confession which Falconer had written in his diary might in some way come to her. Perhaps if it were left here in the bower of honeysuckles where they had so often sat together, it might be a sign and omen of the meeting of these two souls that had lost each other in the dark of the world. Perhaps,—ah, who can tell that it is not so?—for those who truly love, with all their errors, with all their faults, there is no "irrevocable"—there is "another field."

As I turned from the garden, the tense note of the surf vibrated through the night. The pattering drops of dew rustled as they fell from the leaves of the honeysuckle. But underneath these sounds it seemed as if I heard a deep voice saying "Claire!" and a woman's lips whispering "Temple!"

The Keeper of the Light

The Keeper of the Light

At long distance, looking over the blue waters of the
Gulf of St. Lawrence in clear weather, you might think
that you saw a lonely sea-gull, snow-white, perching motionless on a cobble of gray rock. Then, as your boat
drifted in, following the languid tide and the soft southern
breeze, you would perceive that the cobble of rock was a
rugged hill with a few bushes and stunted trees growing
in the crevices, and that the gleaming speck near the
summit must be some kind of a building—if you were on
the coast of Italy or Spain you would say a villa or a farm-
house. Then, as you floated still farther north and drew
nearer to the coast, the desolate hill would detach itself
from the mainland and become a little mountain-isle, with
a flock of smaller islets clustering around it as a brood
of wild ducks keep close to their mother, and with deep
water, nearly two miles wide, flowing between it and the
shore; while the shining speck on the seaward side stood
out clearly as a low, whitewashed dwelling with a sturdy
round tower at one end, crowned with a big eight-sided
lantern—a solitary lighthouse.

That is the Isle of the Wise Virgin. Behind it the long
blue Laurentian Mountains, clothed with unbroken forest, rise in sombre ranges toward the Height of Land.
In front of it the waters of the gulf heave and sparkle far
away to where the dim peaks of St. Anne des Monts are
traced along the southern horizon. Sheltered a little, but
not completely, by the island breakwater of granite, lies
the rocky beach of Dead Men's Point, where an English
navy was wrecked in a night of storm a hundred years
ago.

There are a score of wooden houses, a tiny, weather-
beaten chapel, a Hudson Bay Company's store, a row of

platforms for drying fish, and a varied assortment of boats and nets, strung along the beach now. Dead Men's Point has developed into a centre of industry, with a life, a tradition, a social character of its own. And in one of those houses, as you sit at the door in the lingering June twilight, looking out across the deep channel to where the lantern of the tower is just beginning to glow with orange radiance above the shadow of the island—in that far-away place, in that mystical hour, you should hear the story of the light and its keeper.

I

When the lighthouse was built, many years ago, the island had another name. It was called the Isle of Birds. Thousands of sea-fowl nested there. The handful of people who lived on the shore robbed the nests and slaughtered the birds, with considerable profit. It was perceived in advance that the building of the lighthouse would interfere with this, and with other things. Hence it was not altogether a popular improvement. Marcel Thibault, the oldest inhabitant, was the leader of the opposition.

"That lighthouse!" said he, "what good will it be for us? We know the way in and out when it makes clear weather, by day or by night. But when the sky gets swampy, when it makes fog, then we stay with ourselves at home, or we run into La Trinité, or Pentecôte. We know the way. What? The stranger boats? *B'en!* the stranger boats need not to come here, if they know not the way. The more fish, the more seals, the more everything will there be left for us. Just because of the stranger boats, to build something that makes all the birds wild and spoils the hunting—that is a fool's work. The good God made no stupid light on the Isle of Birds. He saw no necessity of it."

"Besides," continued Thibault, puffing slowly at his pipe, "besides—those stranger boats, sometimes they are lost, they come ashore. It is sad! But who gets the things that are saved, all sorts of things, good to put into our houses, good to eat, good to sell, sometimes a boat that can be patched up almost like new—who gets these things, eh? Doubtless those for whom the good God intended them. But who shall get them when this *sacré* lighthouse is built, eh? Tell me that, you Baptiste Fortin."

Fortin represented the party of progress in the little parliament of the beach. He had come down from Quebec some years ago bringing with him a wife and two little daughters, and a good many new notions about life. He had good luck at the cod-fishing, and built a house with windows at the side as well as in front. When his third girl, Nataline, was born, he went so far as to paint the house red, and put on a kitchen, and enclose a bit of ground for a yard. This marked him as a radical, an innovator. It was expected that he would defend the building of the lighthouse. And he did.

"Monsieur Thibault," he said, "you talk well, but you talk too late. It is of a past age, your talk. A new time comesc to the Côte Nord. We begin to civilize ourselves. To hold back against the light would be our shame. Tell me this, Marcel Thibault, what men are they that love darkness?"

"*Torrieux!*" growled Thibault, "that is a little strong. You say my deeds are evil?"

"No, no," answered Fortin; "I say not that, my friend, but I say this lighthouse means good: good for us, and good for all who come to this coast. It will bring more trade to us. It will bring a boat with the mail, with newspapers, perhaps once, perhaps twice a month, all through the summer. It will bring us into the great world. To lose that for the sake of a few birds—*ça sera b'en de valeur!* Besides, it is impossible. The lighthouse is coming, certain."

Fortin was right, of course. But Thibault's position was not altogether unnatural, nor unfamiliar. All over the world, for the past hundred years, people have been kicking against the sharpness of the pricks that drove them forward out of the old life, the wild life, the free life, grown dear to them because it was so easy. There has been a terrible interference with bird-nesting and other things. All over the world the great Something that bridges rivers, and tunnels mountains, and fells forests, and populates deserts, and opens up the hidden corners of the earth, has been pushing steadily on; and the people who like things to remain as they are have had to give up a great deal. There was no exception made in favour of Dead Men's Point. The Isle of Birds lay in the line of progress. The lighthouse arrived.

It was a very good house for that day. The keeper's dwelling had three rooms and was solidly built. The tower was thirty feet high. The lantern held a revolving light, with a four-wick Presnel lamp, burning sperm oil. There was one of Stevenson's new cages of dioptric prisms around the flame, and once every minute it was turned by clockwork, flashing a broad belt of radiance fifteen miles across the sea. All night long that big bright eye was opening and shutting. *"Baguette!"* said Thibault, "it winks like a one-eyed Windigo."

The Department of Marine and Fisheries sent down an expert from Quebec to keep the light in order and run it for the first summer. He took Fortin as his assistant. By the end of August he reported to headquarters that the light was all right, and that Fortin was qualified to be appointed keeper. Before October was out the certificate of appointment came back, and the expert packed his bag to go up the river.

"Now look here, Fortin," said he, "this is no fishing trip. Do you think you are up to this job?"

"I suppose," said Fortin.

"Well now, do you remember all this business about the machinery that turns the lenses? That's the main thing. The bearings must be kept well oiled, and the weight must never get out of order. The clock-face will tell you when it is running right. If anything gets hitched up here's the crank to keep it going until you can straighten the machine again. It's easy enough to turn it. But you must never let it stop between dark and daylight. The regular turn once a minute—that's the mark of this light. If it shines steady it might as well be out. Yes, better! Any vessel coming along here in a dirty night and seeing a fixed light would take it for the Cap Loup-Marin and run ashore. This particular light has got to revolve once a minute every night from April first to December tenth, certain. Can you do it?"

"Certain," said Fortin.

"That's the way I like to hear a man talk! Now, you've got oil enough to last you through till the tenth of December, when you close the light, and to run on for a month in the spring after you open again. The ice may be late in going out and perhaps the supply-boat can't get down before the middle of April, or thereabouts. But she'll bring plenty of oil when she comes, so you'll be all right."

"All right," said Fortin.

"Well, I've said it all, I guess. You understand what you've got to do? Good-by and good luck. You're the keeper of the light now."

"Good luck," said Fortin,"I am going to keep it."

The same day he shut up the red house on the beach and moved to the white house on the island with Marie-Anne, his wife, and the three girls, Alma, aged seventeen, Azilda, aged fifteen, and Nataline, aged thirteen. He was the captain, and Marie-Anne was the mate, and the three girls were the crew. They were all as full of happy pride as if they had come into possession of a great fortune.

It was the thirty-first day of October. A snow-shower had silvered the island. The afternoon was clear and beautiful. As the sun sloped toward the rose-coloured hills of the mainland the whole family stood out in front of the lighthouse looking up at the tower.

"Regard him well, my children," said Baptiste; "God has given him to us to keep, and to keep us. Thibault says he is a Windigo. *B'en!* We shall see that he is a friendly Windigo. Every minute all the night he shall wing, just for kindness and good luck to all the world, till the day-light."

II

On the ninth of November, at three o'clock in the afternoon, Baptiste went into the tower to see that the clockwork was in order for the night. He set the dial on the machine, put a few drops of oil on the bearings of the cylinder, and started to wind up the weight.

It rose a few inches, gave a dull click, and then stopped dead. He tugged a little harder, but it would not move. Then he tried to let it down. He pushed at the lever that set the clockwork in motion.

He might as well have tried to make the island turn around by pushing at one of the little spruce trees that clung to the rock.

Then it dawned fearfully upon him that something must be wrong. Trembling with anxiety, he climbed up and peered in among the wheels.

The escapement wheel was cracked clean through, as if some one had struck it with the head of an axe, and one of the pallets of the spindle was stuck fast in the crack. He could knock it out easily enough, but when the crack came around again, the pallet would catch and the clock would stop once more. It was a fatal injury.

Baptiste turned white, then red, gripped his head in his hands, and ran down the steps, out of the door, straight toward his canoe, which was pulled up on the western side of the island.

"Dâme!" he cried, "who has done this? Let me catch him! If that old Thibault—"

As he leaped down the rocky slope the setting sun gleamed straight in his eyes. It was poised like a ball of fire on the very edge of the mountains. Five minutes more and darkness would close in. Then the giant's eye must begin to glow, and to wink precisely once a minute all night long. If not, what became of the keeper's word, his faith, his honour?

No matter how the injury to the clockwork was done. No matter who was to be blamed or punished for it. That could wait. The question now was whether the light would fail or not. And it must be answered within a quarter of an hour.

That red ray of the vanishing sun was like a blow in the face to Baptiste. It stopped him short, dazed and bewildered. Then he came to himself, wheeled, and ran up the rocks faster than he had come down.

"Marie-Anne! Alma!" he shouted, as he dashed past the door of the house, "all of you! To me, in the tower!"

He was up in the lantern when they came running in, full of curiosity, excited, asking twenty questions at once. Nataline climbed up the ladder and put her head through the trap-door.

"What is it?" she panted. "What has hap—"

"Go down," answered her father, "go down all at once. Wait for me. I am coming. I will explain."

The explanation was not altogether lucid and scientific. There were some bad words mixed up with it.

Baptiste was still hot with anger and the unsatisfied desire to whip somebody, he did not know whom, for something, he did not know what. But angry as he was, he was still sane enough to hold his mind hard and close to the main point. The crank must be adjusted; the machine must be ready to turn before dark. While he worked he hastily made the situation clear to his listeners.

That crank must be turned by hand, round and round all night, not too slow, not too fast. The dial on the machine must mark time with the clock on the wall. The light must flash once every minute until daybreak. He would do as much of the labour as he could, but the wife and the two older girls must help him. Nataline could go to bed.

At this Nataline's short upper lip trembled. She rubbed her eyes with the sleeve of her dress, and began to weep silently.

"What is the matter with you?" said her mother, "bad child, have you fear to sleep alone? A big girl like you!"

"No," she sobbed, "I have no fear, but I want some of the fun."

"Fun!" growled her father. "What fun? *Nom d'un chien!* She calls this fun!" He looked at her for a moment, as she stood there, half defiant, half despondent, with her red mouth quivering and her big brown eyes sparkling fire; then he burst into a hearty laugh.

"Come here, my little wild-cat," he said, drawing her

to him and kissing her; "you are a good girl after all. I suppose you think this light is part yours, eh?"

The girl nodded.

"*B'en!* You shall have your share, fun and all. You shall make the tea for us and bring us something to eat. Perhaps when Alma and 'Zilda fatigue themselves they will permit a few turns of the crank to you. Are you content? Run now and boil the kettle."

It was a very long night. No matter how easily a handle turns, after a certain number of revolutions there is a stiffness about it. The stiffness is not in the handle, but in the hand that pushes it.

Round and round, evenly, steadily, minute after minute, hour after hour, shoving out, drawing in, circle after circle, no swerving, no stopping, no varying the motion, turn after turn—fifty-five, fifty-six, fifty-seven—what's the use of counting? Watch the dial; go to sleep—no! for God's sake, no sleep! But how hard it is to keep awake! How heavy the arm grows, how stiffly the muscles move, how the will creaks and groans. *Batiscan!* It is not easy for a human being to become part of a machine.

Fortin himself took the longest spell at the crank, of course. He went at his work with a rigid courage. His red-hot anger had cooled down into a shape that was like a bar of forged steel. He meant to make that light revolve if it killed him to do it. He was the captain of a company that had run into an ambuscade. He was going to fight his way through if he had to fight alone.

The wife and the two older girls followed him blindly and bravely, in the habit of sheer obedience. They did not quite understand the meaning of the task, the honour of victory, the shame of defeat. But Fortin said it must be done, and he knew best. So they took their places in turn, as he grew weary, and kept the light flashing.

And Nataline—well, there is no way of describing what Nataline did, except to say that she played the fife.

She felt the contest just as her father did, not as deeply, perhaps, but in the same spirit. She went into the fight with darkness like a little soldier. And she played the fife.

When she came up from the kitchen with the smoking

pail of tea, she rapped on the door and called out to know whether the Windigo was at home to-night.

She ran in and out of the place like a squirrel. She looked up at the light and laughed. Then she ran in and reported. "He winks," she said, "old one-eye winks beautifully. Keep him going. My turn now!"

She refused to be put off with a shorter spell than the other girls. "No," she cried, "I can do it as well as you. You think you are so much older. Well, what of that? The light is part mine; father said so. Let me turn. *Va-t-en.*"

When the first glimmer of the little day came shivering along the eastern horizon, Nataline was at the crank. The mother and the two older girls were half asleep. Baptiste stepped out to look at the sky. "Come," he cried, returning. "We can stop now, it is growing gray in the east, almost morning."

"But not yet," said Nataline; "we must wait for the first red. A few more turns. Let's finish it up with a song."

She shook her head and piped up the refrain of the old Canadian *chanson*:

> *En roulant ma boule-le roulant*
> *En roulant ma bou-le.*

And to that cheerful music the first night's battle was carried through to victory.

The next day Fortin spent two hours in trying to repair the clockwork. It was of no use. The broken part was indispensable and could not be replaced.

At noon he went over to the mainland to tell of the disaster, and perhaps to find out if any hostile hand was responsible for it. He found out nothing. Every one denied all knowledge of the accident. Perhaps there was a flaw in the wheel; perhaps it had broken itself. That was possible. Fortin could not deny it; but the thing that hurt him most was that he got so little sympathy. Nobody seemed to care whether the light was kept burning or not. When he told them how the machine had been turned all night by hand, they were astonished. "*Cré-ié!*" they cried, "you must have had a great misery to do that." But that he proposed to go on doing it for a month longer, until

December tenth, and to begin again on April first, and go on turning the light by hand for three or four weeks more until the supply-boat came down and brought the necessary tools to repair the machine—such an idea as this went beyond their horizon.

"But you are crazy, Baptiste," they said, "you can never do it; you are not capable."

"I would be crazy," he answered, "if I did not see what I must do. That light is my charge. In all the world there is nothing else so great as that for me and for my family —you understand? For us it is the chief thing. It is my Ten Commandments. I shall keep it or be damned."

There was a silence after this remark. They were not very particular about the use of language at Dead Men's Point, but this shocked them a little. They thought that Fortin was swearing a shade too hard. In reality he was never more reverent, never more soberly in earnest.

After a while he continued, "I want some one to help me with the work on the island. We must be up all the nights now. By day we must get some sleep. I want another man or a strong boy. Is there any who will come? The Government will pay. Or if not, I will pay, *moi-même*"

There was no response. All the men hung back. The lighthouse was still unpopular, or at least it was on trial. Fortin's pluck and resolution had undoubtedly impressed them a little. But they still hesitated to commit themselves to his side.

"*B'en,*" he said, "there is no one. Then we shall manage the affair *en famille. Bon soir, messieurs!*"

He walked down to the beach with his head in the air, without looking back. But before he had his canoe in the water he heard some one running down behind him. It was Thibault's youngest son, Marcel, a well-grown boy of sixteen, very much out of breath with running and shyness.

"Monsieur Fortin," he stammered, "will you—do you think—am I big enough?"

Baptiste looked him in the face for a moment. Then his eyes twinkled.

"Certain," he answered, "you are bigger than your father. But what will he say to this?"

"He says," blurted out Marcel—"well, he says that he will say nothing if I do not ask him."

So the little Marcel was enlisted in the crew on the island. For thirty nights those six people—a man, and a boy, and four women (Nataline was not going to submit to any distinctions on the score of age, you may be sure)—for a full month they turned their flashing lantern by hand from dusk to daybreak.

The fog, the frost, the hail, the snow beleagured their tower. Hunger and cold, sleeplessness and weariness, pain and discouragement, held rendezvous in that dismal, cramped little room. Many a night Nataline's fife of fun played a feeble, wheezy note. But it played. And the crank went round. And every bit of glass in the lantern was as clear as polished crystal. And the big lamp was full of oil. And the great eye of the friendly giant winked without ceasing, through fierce storm and placid moonlight.

When the tenth of December came, the light went to sleep for the winter, and the keepers took their way across the ice to the mainland. They had won the battle, not only on the island, fighting against the elements, but also at Dead Men's Point, against public opinion. The inhabitants began to understand that the lighthouse meant something—a law, an order, a principle.

Men cannot help feeling respect for a thing when they see others willing to fight or to suffer for it.

When the time arrived to kindle the light again in the spring, Fortin could have had any one that he wanted to help him. But no; he chose the little Marcel again; the boy wanted to go, and he had earned the right. Besides, he and Nataline had struck up a close friendship on the island, cemented during the winter by various hunting excursions after hares and ptarmigan. Marcel was a skilful setter of snares. But Nataline was not content until she had won consent to borrow her father's *carabine*. They hunted in partnership. One day they had shot a fox. That is, Nataline had shot it, though Marcel had seen it first and tracked it. Now they wanted to try for a seal on the point of the island when the ice went out. It was quite essential that Marcel should go.

"Besides," said Baptiste to his wife, confidentially, "a boy costs less than a man. Why should we waste money? Marcel is best."

A peasant-hero is seldom averse to economy in small things, like money.

But there was not much play in the spring session with the light on the island. It was a bitter job. December had been lamb-like compared with April. First, the southeast wind kept the ice driving in along the shore. Then the northwest wind came hurtling down from the Arctic wilderness like a pack of wolves. There was a snow-storm of four days and nights that made the whole world— earth and sky and sea—look like a crazy white chaos. And through it all, that weary, dogged crank must be kept turning—turning from dark to daylight.

It seemed as if the supply-boat would never come. At last they saw it, one fair afternoon, April the twenty-ninth, creeping slowly down the coast. They were just getting ready for another night's work.

Fortin ran out of the tower, took off his hat, and began to say his prayers. The wife and the two elder girls stood in the kitchen door, crossing themselves, with tears in their eyes. Marcel and Nataline were coming up from the point of the island, where they had been watching for their seal. She was singing

> *Mon père n'avait fille que moi,*
> *Encore sur la mer il m'envoi-e-eh!*

When she saw the boat she stopped short for a minute.

"Well," she said, "they find us awake, *n'est-c'pas?* And if they don't come faster than that we'll have another chance to show them how we make the light wink, eh?"

Then she went on with her song—

> *Sautez, mignonne, Cécilia.*
> *Ah, ah, ah, ah, Cécilia!*

III

You did not suppose that was the end of the story, did you?

No, an out-of-doors story does not end like that, broken off in the middle, with a bit of a song. It goes on to something definite, like a wedding or a funeral.

You have not heard, yet, how near the light came to failing, and how the keeper saved it and something else too. Nataline's story is not told; it is only begun. This first part is only the introduction, just to let you see what kind of a girl she was, and how her life was made. If you want to hear the conclusion, we must hurry along a little faster or we shall never get to it.

Nataline grew up like a young birch tree—stately and strong, good to look at. She was beautiful in her place; she fitted it exactly. Her bronzed face with an undertinge of red; her low, black eyebrows; her clear eyes like the brown waters of a woodland stream; her dark, curly hair with little tendrils always blowing loose around the pillar of her neck; her broad breast and sloping shoulders; her firm, fearless step; her voice, rich and vibrant; her straight, steady looks—but there, who can describe a thing like that? I tell you she was a girl to love out-of-doors.

There was nothing that she could not do. She could cook; she could swing an axe; she could paddle a canoe; she could fish; she could shoot; and, best of all, she could run the lighthouse. Her father's devotion to it had gone into her blood. It was the centre of her life, her law of God. There was nothing about it that she did not understand and love. From the first of April to the tenth of December the flashing of that light was like the beating of her heart—steady, even, unfaltering. She kept time to it as unconsciously as the tides follow the moon. She lived by it and for it.

There were no more accidents to the clockwork after

the first one was repaired. It ran on regularly, year after year.

Alma and Azilda were married and went away to live, one on the South Shore, the other at Quebec. Nataline was her father's right-hand man. As the rheumatism took hold of him and lamed his shoulders and wrists, more and more of the work fell upon her. She was proud of it.

At last it came to pass, one day in January, that Baptiste died. He was not gathered to his fathers, for they were buried far away beside the Montmorenci, and on the rocky coast of Brittany. But the men dug through the snow behind the tiny chapel at Dead Men's Point, and made a grave for Baptiste Fortin, and the young priest of the mission read the funeral service over it.

It went without saying that Nataline was to be the keeper of the light, at least until the supply-boat came down again in the spring and orders arrived from the Government in Quebec. Why not? She was a woman, it is true. But if a woman can do a thing as well as a man, why should she not do it? Besides, Nataline could do this particular thing much better than any man on the Point. Everybody approved of her as the heir of her father, especially young Marcel Thibault.

What?

Yes, of course. You could not help guessing it. He was Nataline's lover. They were to be married the next summer. They sat together in the best room, while the old mother was rocking to and fro and knitting beside the kitchen stove, and talked of what they were going to do. Once in a while, when Nataline grieved for her father, she would let Marcel put his arm around her and comfort her in the way that lovers know. But their talk was mainly of the future, because they were young, and of the light, because Nataline's life belonged to it.

Perhaps the Government would remember that year when it was kept going by hand for two months, and give it to her to keep as long as she lived. That would be only fair. Certainly, it was hers for the present. No one had as good a right to it. She took possession without a doubt. At all events, while she was the keeper the light should not fail.

But that winter was a bad one on the North Shore, and particularly at Dead Men's Point. It was terribly bad. The summer before, the fishing had been almost a dead failure. In June a wild storm had smashed all the salmon nets and swept most of them away. In July they could find no caplin for bait for the cod-fishing, and in August and September they could find no cod. The few bushels of potatoes that some of the inhabitants had planted, rotted in the ground. The people at the Point went into the winter short of money and very short of food.

There were some supplies at the store, pork and flour and molasses, and they could run through the year on credit and pay their debts the following summer if the fish came back. But this resource also failed them. In the last week of January the store caught fire and burned up. Nothing was saved. The only hope now was the seal-hunting in February and March and April. That at least would bring them meat and oil enough to keep them from starvation.

But this hope failed, too. The winds blew strong from the north and west, driving the ice far out into the gulf. The chase was long and perilous. The seals were few and wild. Less than a dozen were killed in all. By the last week in March Dead Men's Point stood face to face with famine.

Then it was that old Thibault had an idea.

"There is sperm oil on the Island of Birds," said he, "in the lighthouse, plenty of it, gallons of it. It is not very good to taste, perhaps, but what of that? It will keep life in the body. The Esquimaux drink it in the north, often. We must take the oil of the lighthouse to keep us from starving until the supply-boat comes down."

"But how shall we get it?" asked the others. "It is locked up. Nataline Fortin has the key. Will she give it?"

"Give it?" growled Thibault. "Name of a name! of course she will give it. She must. Is not a life, the life of all of us, more than a light?"

A self-appointed committee of three, with Thibault at

the head, waited upon Nataline without delay, told her their plan, and asked for the key. She thought it over silently for a few minutes, and then refused point-blank.

"No," she said, "I will not give the key. That oil is for the lamp. If you take it, the lamp will not be lighted on the first of April; it will not be burning when the supply-boat comes. For me, that would be shame, disgrace, worse than death. I am the keeper of the light. You shall not have the oil."

They argued with her, pleaded with her, tried to browbeat her. She was a rock. Her round under-jaw was set like a steel trap. Her lips straightened into a white line. Her eyebrows drew together, and her eyes grew black.

"No," she cried, "I tell you no, no, a thousand times no. All in this house I will share with you. But not one drop of what belongs to the light! Never!"

Later in the afternoon the priest came to see her; a thin, pale young man, bent with the hardships of his life, and with sad dreams in his sunken eyes. He talked with her very gently and kindly.

"Think well, my daughter; think seriously what you do. Is it not our first duty to save human life? Surely that must be according to the will of God. Will you refuse to obey it?"

Nataline was trembling a little now. Her brows were unlocked. The tears stood in her eyes and ran down her cheeks. She was twisting her hands together.

"My father," she answered, "I desire to do the will of God. But how shall I know it? Is it not His first command that we should love and serve Him faithfully in the duty which He has given us? He gave me this light to keep. My father kept it. He is dead. If I am unfaithful what will he say to me? Besides, the supply-boat is coming soon—I have thought of this—when it comes it will bring food. But if the light is out, the boat may be lost. That would be the punishment for my sin. No, *mon père,* we must trust God. He will keep the people. I will keep the light."

The priest looked at her long and steadily. A glow came into his face. He put his hand on her shoulder. "You shall follow your conscience," he said quietly. "Peace be with you, Nataline."

That evening just at dark Marcel came. She let him take her in his arms and kiss her. She felt like a little child, tired and weak.

"Well," he whispered, "you have done bravely, sweetheart. You were right not to give the key. That would have been a shame to you. But it is all settled now. They will have the oil without your fault. To-night they are going out to the lighthouse to break in and take what they want. You need not know. There will be no blame—"

She straightened in his arms as if an electric shock had passed through her. She sprang back, blazing with anger.

"What?" she cried, "me a thief by round-about,—with my hand behind my back and my eyes shut? Never. Do you think I care only for the blame? I tell you that is nothing. My light shall not be robbed, never, never!"

She came close to him and took him by the shoulders. Their eyes were on a level. He was a strong man, but she was the stronger then.

"Marcel Thibault," she said, "do you love me?"

"My faith," he gasped, "I do. You know I do."

"Then listen," she continued; "this is what you are going to do. You are going down to the shore at once to make ready the big canoe. I am going to get food enough to last us for the month. It will be a hard pinch, but it will do. Then we are going out to the island to-night, in less than an hour. Day after to-morrow is the first of April. Then we shall light the lantern, and it shall burn every night until the boat comes down. You hear? Now go: and be quick: and bring your gun."

IV

They pushed off in the black darkness, among the fragments of ice that lay along the shore. They crossed the strait in silence, and hid their canoe among the rocks on the island. They carried their stuff up to the house and locked it in the kitchen. Then they unlocked the tower, and went in, Marcel with his shot-gun, and Nataline with her father's old *carabine*. They fastened the door again, and bolted it, and sat down in the dark to wait.

Presently they heard the grating of the prow of the barge on the stones below, the steps of men stumbling up the steep path, and voices mingled in confused talk. The glimmer of a couple of lanterns went bobbing in and out among the rocks and bushes. There was a little crowd of eight or ten men, and they came on carelessly, chattering and laughing. Three of them carried axes, and three others a heavy log of wood which they had picked up on their way.

"The log is better than the axes," said one; "take it in your hands this way, two of you on one side, another on the opposite side in the middle. Then swing it back and forwards and let it go. The door will come down, I tell you, like a sheet of paper. But wait till I give the word, then swing hard. One—two—"

"Stop!" cried Nataline, throwing open the little window. "If you dare to touch that door, I shoot."

She thrust out the barrel of the rifle, and Marcel's shot-gun appeared beside it. The old rifle was not loaded, but who knew that? Besides, both barrels of the shot-gun were full.

There was amazement in the crowd outside the tower, and consternation, and then anger.

"Marcel," they shouted, "you there? *Maudit polisson!* Come out of that. Let us in. You told us—"

"I know," answered Marcel, "but I was mistaken, that is all. I stand by Mademoiselle Fortin. What she says is right. If any man tries to break in here, we kill him. No more talk!"

The gang muttered; cursed; threatened; looked at the guns; and went off to their boat.

"It is murder that you will do," one of them called out, "you are a murderess, you Mademoiselle Fortin! you cause the people to die of hunger!"

"Not I," she answered; "that is as the good God pleases. No matter. The light shall burn."

They heard the babble of the men as they stumbled

down the hill; the grinding of the boat on the rocks as they shoved off; the rattle of the oars in the rowlocks. After that the island was as still as a graveyard.

Then Nataline sat down on the floor in the dark, and put her face in her hands, and cried. Marcel tried to comfort her. She took his hand and pushed it gently away from her waist.

"No, Marcel," she said, "not now! Not that, please, Marcel! Come into the house. I want to talk with you."

They went into the cold, dark kitchen, lit a candle and kindled a fire in the stove. Nataline busied herself with a score of things. She put away the poor little store of provisions, sent Marcel for a pail of water, made some tea, spread the table, and sat down opposite to him. For a time she kept her eyes turned away from him, while she talked about all sorts of things. Then she fell silent for a little, still not looking at him. She got up and moved about the room, arranged two or three packages on the shelves, shut the damper of the stove, glancing at Marcel's back out of the corners of her eyes. Then she came back to her chair, pushed her cup aside, rested both elbows on the table and her chin in her hands, and looked Marcel square in the face with her clear brown eyes.

"My friend," she said, "are you an honest man, *un brave garçon?*"

For an instant he could say nothing. He was so puzzled. "Why yes, Nataline," he answered, "yes, surely—I hope."

"Then let me speak to you without fear," she continued. "You do not suppose that I am ignorant of what I have done this night. I am not a baby. You are a man. I am a girl. We are shut up alone in this house for two weeks, a month, God knows how long. You know what that means, what people will say. I have risked all that a girl has most precious. I have put my good name in your hands."

Marcel tried to speak, but she stopped him.

"Let me finish. It is not easy to say. I know you are honourable. I trust you waking and sleeping. But I am a woman. There must be no love-making. We have other work to do. The light must not fail. You will not touch me, you will not embrace me—not once—till after the boat has come. Then"—she smiled at him like a sun-burned angel—"well, is it a bargain?"

She put out one hand across the table. Marcel took it in both of his own. He did not kiss it. He lifted it up in front of his face.

"I swear to you, Nataline, you shall be to me as the Blessed Virgin herself."

The next day they put the light in order, and the following night they kindled it. They still feared another attack from the mainland, and thought it needful that one of them should be on guard all the time, though the machine itself was working beautifully and needed little watching. Nataline took the night duty; it was her own choice; she loved the charge of the lamp. Marcel was on duty through the day. They were together for three or four hours in the morning and in the evening.

It was not a desperate vigil like that affair with the broken clockwork eight years before. There was no weary turning of the crank. There was just enough work to do about the house and the tower to keep them busy. The weather was fair. The worst thing was the short supply of food. But though they were hungry, they were not starving. And Nataline still played the fife. She jested, she sang, she told long fairy stories while they sat in the kitchen. Marcel admitted that it was not at all a bad arrangement.

But his thoughts turned very often to the arrival of the supply-boat. He hoped it would not be late. The ice was well broken up already and driven far out into the gulf. The boat ought to be able to run down the shore in good time.

One evening as Nataline came down from her sleep she saw Marcel coming up the rocks dragging a young seal behind him.

"Hurra!" he shouted, "here is plenty of meat. I shot it out at the end of the island, about an hour ago.

But Nataline said that they did not need the seal. There was still food enough in the larder. On shore there must be greater need. Marcel must take the seal over to the mainland that night and leave it on the beach near the priest's house. He grumbled a little, but he did it.

That was on the twenty-third of April. The clear sky held for three days longer, calm, bright, halcyon weather. On the afternoon of the twenty-seventh the clouds came down from the north, not a long furious tempest, but a brief, sharp storm, with considerable wind and a whirling, blinding fall of April snow. It was a bad night for boats at sea, confusing, bewildering, a night when the lighthouse had to do its best. Nataline was in the tower all night, tending the lamp, watching the clockwork. Once it seemed to her that the lantern was so covered with snow that light could not shine through. She got her long brush and scraped the snow away. It was cold work, but she gloried in it. The bright eye of the tower, winking, winking steadily through the storm seemed to be the sign of her power in the world. It was hers. She kept it shining.

When morning came the wind was still blowing fitfully off shore, but the snow had almost ceased. Nataline stopped the clockwork, and was just climbing up into the lantern to put out the lamp, when Marcel's voice hailed her.

"Come down, Nataline, come down quick. Make haste!"

She turned and hurried out, not knowing what was to come; perhaps a message of trouble from the mainland, perhaps a new assault on the lighthouse.

As she came out of the tower, her brown eyes heavy from the night-watch, her dark face pale from the cold, she saw Marcel standing on the rocky knoll beside the house and pointing shoreward.

She ran up beside him and looked. There, in the deep water between the island and the point, lay the supply-boat, rocking quietly on the waves.

It flashed upon her in a moment what it meant—the end of her fight, relief for the village, victory! And the light that had guided the little ship safe through the stormy night into the harbour was hers.

She turned and looked up at the lamp, still burning.

"I kept you!" she cried.

Then she turned to Marcel; the colour rose quickly in her cheeks, the light sparkled in her eyes; she smiled, and held out both her hands, whispering, "Now you shall keep me!"

There was a fine wedding on the last day of April, and from that time the island took its new name,—the Isle of the Wise Virgin.

Little Rivers

Little Rivers

'There's no music like a little river's. It plays the same tune (and that's the favourite) over and over again, and yet does not weary of it like men fiddlers. It takes the mind out of doors; and though we should be grateful for good houses, there is, after all, no house like God's out-of-doors. And lastly, sir, it quiets a man down like saying his prayers.'—ROBERT LOUIS STEVENSON: *Prince Otto.*

A river is the most human and companionable of all inanimate things. It has a life, a character, a voice of its own, and is as full of good fellowship as a sugar-maple is of sap. It can talk in various tones, loud or low, and of many subjects, grave and gay. Under favourable circumstances it will even make a shift to sing, not in a fashion that can be reduced to notes and set down in black and white on a sheet of paper, but in a vague, refreshing manner, and to a wandering air that goes

Over the hills and far away.

For real company and friendship, there is nothing outside of the animal kingdom that is comparable to a river.

I will admit that a very good case can be made out in favour of some other objects of natural affection. For example, a fair apology has been offered by those ambitious persons who have fallen in love with the sea. But, after all, that is a formless and disquieting passion. It lacks solid comfort and mutual confidence. The sea is too big for loving, and too uncertain. It will not fit into our thoughts. It has no personality because it has so many.

It is a salt abstraction. You might as well think of loving a glittering generality like "the American woman." One would be more to the purpose.

Mountains are more satisfying because they are more individual. It is possible to feel a very strong attachment for a certain range whose outline has grown familiar to our eyes, or a clear peak that has looked down, day after day, upon our joys and sorrows, moderating our passions with its calm aspect. We come back from our travels, and the sight of such a well-known mountain is like meeting an old friend unchanged. But it is a one-sided affection. The mountain is voiceless and imperturbable; and its very loftiness and serenity sometimes make us the more lonely.

Trees seem to come closer to our life. They are often rooted in our richest feelings, and our sweetest memories, like birds, build nests in their branches. I remember, the last time that I saw James Russell Lowell, (only a few weeks before his musical voice was hushed,) he walked out with me into the quiet garden at Elmwood to say good-bye. There was a great horse-chestnut tree beside the house, towering above the gable, and covered with blossoms from base to summit,—a pyramid of green supporting a thousand smaller pyramids of white. The poet looked up at it with his gray, pain-furrowed face, and laid his trembling hand upon the trunk. "I planted the nut," said he, "from which this tree grew. And my father was with me and showed me how to plant it."

Yes, there is a good deal to be said in behalf of tree-worship; and when I recline with my friend Tityrus beneath the shade of his favourite oak, I consent in his devotions. But when I invite him with me to share my orisons, or wander alone to indulge the luxury of grateful, unlaborious thought, my feet turn not to a tree, but to the bank of a river, for there the musings of solitude find a friendly accompaniment, and human intercourse is purified and sweetened by the flowing, murmuring water. It is by a river that I would choose to make love, and to revive old friendships, and to play with the children, and to confess my faults, and to escape from vain, selfish desires, and to cleanse my mind from all the false and foolish things that mar the joy and peace of living. Like David's hart, I pant for the water-brooks, and would follow the advice of Seneca, who says, "Where a spring rises, or a river flows, there should we build altars and offer sacrifices."

The personality of a river is not to be found in its water, nor in its bed, nor in its shore. Either of these elements, by itself, would be nothing. Confine the fluid contents of the noblest stream in a walled channel of stone, and it ceases to be a stream; it becomes what Charles Lamb calls "a mockery of a river—a liquid artifice—a wretched conduit." But take away the water from the most beautiful river-banks, and what is left? An ugly road with none to travel it; a long, ghastly scar on the bosom of the earth.

The life of a river, like that of a human being, consists in the union of soul and body, the water and the banks. They belong together. They act and react upon each other. The stream moulds and makes the shore; hollowing out a bay here, and building a long point there; alluring the little bushes close to its side, and bending the tall slim trees over its current; sweeping a rocky ledge clean of everything but moss, and sending a still lagoon full of white arrow-heads and rosy knot-weed far back into the meadow. The shore guides and controls the stream; now detaining and now advancing it; now bending it in a hundred sinuous curves, and now speeding it straight as a wild-bee on its homeward flight; here hiding the water in a deep cleft overhung with green branches, and there spreading it out, like a mirror framed in daises, to reflect the sky and the clouds; sometimes breaking it with sudden turns and unexpected falls into a foam of musical laughter, sometimes soothing it into a sleepy motion like the flow of a dream.

And is it otherwise with the men and women whom we know and like? Does not the spirit influence the form, and the form affect the spirit? Can we divide and separate them in our affections?

I am no friend to purely psychological attachments.

In some unknown future they may be satisfying, but in the present I want your words and your voice, with your thoughts, your looks and your gestures, to interpret your feelings. The warm, strong grasp of Greatheart's hand is as dear to me as the steadfast fashion of his friendships; the lively, sparkling eyes of the master of Rudder Grange charm me as much as the nimbleness of his fancy; and the firm poise of the Hoosier Schoolmaster's shaggy head gives me new confidence in the solidity of his views of life. I like the pure tranquillity of Isabel's brow as well as her

> most silver flow
> Of subtle-pacèd counsel in distress

The soft cadences and turns in my lady Katrina's speech draw me into the humour of her gentle judgments of men and things. The touches of quaintness in Angelica's dress, her folded kerchief and smooth-parted hair, seem to partake of herself, and enhance my admiration for the sweet order of her thoughts and her old-fashioned ideals of love and duty. Even so the stream and its channel are one life, and I cannot think of the swift, brown flood of the Batiscan without its shadowing primeval forests, or the crystalline current of the Boquet without its beds of pebbles and golden sand and grassy banks embroidered with flowers.

Every country—or at least every country that is fit for habitation—has its own rivers; and every river has its own quality; and it is the part of wisdom to know and love as many as you can, seeing each in the fairest possible light, and receiving from each the best that it has to give. The torrents of Norway leap down from their mountain homes with plentiful cataracts, and run brief but glorious races to the sea. The streams of England move smoothly through green fields and beside ancient, sleepy towns. The Scotch rivers brawl through the open moorland and flash along steep Highland glens. The rivers of the Alps are born in icy caves, from which they issue forth with furious, turbid waters; but when their anger has been forgotten in the slumber of some blue lake, they flow down more softly to see the vineyards of France and Italy, the gray castles of Germany, and the verdant meadows of Holland. The mighty rivers of the West roll their yellow floods through broad valleys, or plunge down dark cañons. The rivers of the South creep under dim arboreal archways heavy with banners of waving moss. The Delaware and the Hudson and the Connecticut are the children of the Catskills and the Adirondacks and the White Mountains, cradled among the forests of spruce and hemlock, playing through a wild woodland youth, gathering strength from numberless tributaries to bear their great burdens of lumber and turn the wheels of many mills, issuing from the hills to water a thousand farms, and descending at last, beside new cities, to the ancient sea.

Every river that flows is good, and has something worthy to be loved. But those that we love most are always the ones that we have known best,—the stream that ran before our father's door, the current on which we ventured our first boat or cast our first fly, the brook on whose banks we first picked the twinflower of young love. However far we may travel, we come back to Naaman's state of mind: "Are not Abana and Pharpar, rivers of Damascus, better than all the waters of Israel?"

It is with rivers as it is with people: the greatest are not always the most agreeable, nor the best to live with. Diogenes must have been an uncomfortable bedfellow: Antinoüs was bored to death in the society of the Emperor Hadrian: and you can imagine much better company for a walking-trip than Napoleon Bonaparte. Semiramis was a lofty queen, but I fancy that Ninus had more than one bad quarter-of-an-hour with her: and in "the spacious times of great Elizabeth" there was many a milkmaid whom the wise man would have chosen for his friend, before the royal red-haired virgin. "I confess," says the poet Cowley, "I love Littleness almost in all things. A little convenient Estate, a little chearful House, a little Company, and a very little Feast, and if I were ever to fall in Love again, (which is a great Passion, and therefore, I hope, I have done with it,) it would be, I think, with Prettiness, rather than with Majestical Beauty. I would neither wish that my Mistress, nor my Fortune, should be a *Bona Roba*, as *Homer* uses to describe his Beauties, like a daughter of great *Jupiter* for the stateliness and largeness of her Person, but as *Lucretius* says:

'*Parvula, pumilio*, Χαρίτων μία, *tota merum sal.*' "

Now in talking about women it is prudent to disguise a prejudice like this, in the security of a dead language, and to entrench it behind a fortress of reputable authority. But in lowlier and less dangerous matters, such as we are now concerned with, one may dare to speak in plain English. I am all for the little rivers. Let those who will, chant in heroic verse the renown of Amazon and Mississippi and Niagara, but my prose shall flow—or straggle along at such a pace as the prosaic muse may grant me to attain—in praise of Beaverkill and Neversink and Swiftwater, of Saranac and Raquette and Ausable, of Allegash and Aroostook and Moose River. "Whene'er I take my walks abroad," it shall be to trace the clear Rauma from its rise on the *fjeld* to its rest in the *fjord*; or to follow the Ericht and the Halladale through the heather. The Ziller and the Salzach shall be my guides through the Tyrol; the Rotha and the Dove shall lead me into the heart of England. My sacrificial flames shall be kindled with birchbark along the wooded stillwaters of the Penobscot and the Peribonca, and my libations drawn from the pure current of the Ristigouche and the Ampersand, and my altar of remembrance shall rise upon the rocks beside the falls of Seboomok.

I will set my affections upon rivers that are not too great for intimacy. And if by chance any of these little ones have also become famous, like the Tweed and the Thames and the Arno, I at least will praise them, because they are still at heart little rivers.

If an open fire is, as Charles Dudley Warner says, the eye of a room; then surely a little river may be called the mouth, the most expressive feature, of a landscape. It animates and enlivens the whole scene. Even a railway journey becomes tolerable when the track follows the course of a running stream.

What charming glimpses you catch from the window as the train winds along the valley of the French Broad from Asheville, or climbs the southern Catskills beside the Æsopus, or slides down the Pusterthal with the Rienz, or follows the Glommen and the Gula from Christiania to Throndhjem. Here is a mill with its dripping, lazy wheel, the type of somnolent industry; and there is a white cascade, foaming in silent pantomime as the train clatters by; and here is a long, still pool with the cows standing knee-deep in the water and swinging their tails in calm indifference to the passing world; and there is a lone fisherman sitting upon a rock, rapt in contemplation of the point of his rod. For a moment you become the partner of his tranquil enterprise. You turn around, you crane your neck to get the last sight of his motionless angle. You do not know what kind of fish he expects to catch, nor what species of bait he is using, but at least you pray that he may have a bite before the train swings around the next curve. And if perchance your wish is granted, and you see him gravely draw some unknown, reluctant, shining reward of patience from the water, you feel like swinging your hat from the window and crying out "Good luck!"

Little rivers seem to have the indefinable quality that belongs to certain people in the world,—the power of drawing attention without courting it, the faculty of exciting interest by their very presence and way of doing things.

The most fascinating part of a city or town is that through which the water flows. Idlers always choose a bridge for their place of meditation when they can get it; and, failing that, you will find them sitting on the edge of a quay or embankment, with their feet hanging over the water. What a piquant mingling of indolence and vivacity you can enjoy by the river-side! The best point of view in Rome, to my taste, is the Ponte San Angelo; and in Florence or Pisa I never tire of loafing along the Lung' Arno. You do not know London until you have seen it from the Thames. And you will miss the charm of Cambridge unless you take a little boat and go drifting on the placid Cam, beneath the bending trees, along the backs of the colleges.

But the real way to know a little river is not to glance at it here or there in the course of a hasty journey, nor to become acquainted with it after it has been partly civilized and partly spoiled by too close contact with the works of man. You must go to its native haunts; you must see it in youth and freedom; you must accommodate yourself to its pace, and give yourself to its influence, and follow its meanderings whithersoever they may lead you.

Now, of this pleasant pastime there are three principal forms. You may go as a walker, taking the river-side path, or making a way for yourself through the tangled thickets or across the open meadows. You may go as a sailor, launching your light canoe on the swift current and committing yourself for a day, or a week, or a month, to the delightful uncertainties of a voyage through the forest. You may go as a wader, stepping into the stream and going down with it, through rapids and shallows and deeper pools, until you come to the end of your courage and the daylight. Of these three ways I know not which is best. But in all of them the essential thing is that you must be willing and glad to be led; you must take the little river for your guide, philosopher, and friend.

And what a good guidance it gives you. How cheerfully it lures you on into the secrets of field and wood, and brings you acquainted with the birds and the flowers. The stream can show you, better than any other teacher, how nature works her enchantments with colour and music.

Go out to the Beaver-kill

In the tassel-time of spring,

and follow its brimming waters through the budding forests, to that corner which we call the Painter's Camp. See how the banks are all enamelled with the pale hepatica, the painted trillium, and the delicate pink-veined spring beauty. A little later in the year, when the ferns are uncurling their long fronds, the troops of blue and white violets will come dancing down to the edge of the stream, and creep venturously out to the very end of that long, moss-covered log in the water. Before these have vanished, the yellow crow-foot and the cinquefoil will appear, followed by the star-grass and the loose-strife and the golden St. John's-wort. Then the unseen painter begins to mix the royal colour on his palette, and the red of the bee-balm catches your eye. If you are lucky, you may find, in midsummer, a slender fragrant spike of the purple-fringed orchis, and you cannot help finding the universal self-heal. Yellow returns in the drooping flowers of the jewel-weed, and blue repeats itself in the trembling hare-bells, and scarlet is glorified in the flaming robe of the cardinal-flower. Later still, the summer closes in a splendour of bloom, with gentians and asters and golden-rod.

You never get so close to the birds as when you are wading quietly down a little river, casting your fly deftly under the branches for the wary trout, but ever on the lookout for all the various pleasant things that nature has to bestow upon you. Here you shall come upon the cat-bird at her morning bath, and hear her sing, in a clump of pussy-willows, that low, tender, confidential song which she keeps for the hours of domestic intimacy. The spotted sandpiper will run along the stones before you, crying, *"wet-feet, wet-feet!"* and bowing and teetering in the friendliest manner, as if to show you the way to the best pools. In the thick branches of the hemlocks that stretch across the stream, the tiny warblers, dressed in a hundred colours, chirp and twitter confidingly above your head; and the Maryland yellow-throat, flitting through the bushes like a little gleam of sunlight, calls *"witchery, witchery, witchery!"* That plaintive, forsaken, persistent note, never ceasing, even in the noonday silence, comes from the wood-pewee, drooping upon the bough of some high tree, and complaining, like Mariana in the moated grange, *"weary, weary, wéary!"*

When the stream runs out into the old clearing, or down through the pasture, you find other and livelier birds,—

the robin, with his sharp, saucy call and breathless, merry warble; the bluebird, with his notes of pure gladness, and the oriole, with his wild, flexible whistle; the chewink, bustling about in the thicket, talking to his sweetheart in French, "*chérie, chérie!*" and the song-sparrow, perched on his favourite limb of a young maple, close beside the water, and singing happily, through sunshine and through rain. This is the true bird of the brook, after all, the winged spirit of cheerfulness and contentment, the patron saint of little rivers, the fisherman's friend. He seems to enter into your sport with his good wishes, and for an hour at a time, while you are trying every fly in your book, from a black gnat to a white miller, to entice the crafty old trout at the foot of the meadow-pool, the song-sparrow, close above you, will be chanting patience and encouragement. And when at last success crowns your endeavour, and the parti-coloured prize is glittering in your net, the bird on the bough breaks out in an ecstasy of congratulation: "*catch 'im, catch 'im, catch 'im; oh, what a pretty fellow! sweet!*"

There are other birds that seem to have a very different temper. The blue-jay sits high up in the withered-pine tree, bobbing up and down, and calling to his mate in a tone of affected sweetness, "*salúte-her, salúte-her,*" but when you come in sight he flies away with a harsh cry of "*thief, thief, thief!*" The kingfisher, ruffling his crest in solitary pride on the end of a dead branch, darts down the stream at your approach, winding up his reel angrily as if he despised you for interrupting his fishing. And the cat-bird, that sang so charmingly while she thought herself unobserved, now tries to scare you away by screaming "*snake, snake!*"

As evening draws near, and the light beneath the trees grows yellower, and the air is full of filmy insects out for their last dance, the voice of the little river becomes louder and more distinct. The true poets have often noticed this apparent increase in the sound of flowing waters at nightfall. Gray, in one of his letters, speaks of "hearing the murmur of many waters not audible in the daytime." Wordsworth repeats the same thought almost in the same words:

> A soft and lulling sound is heard
> Of streams inaudible by day.

And Tennyson, in the valley of Cauteretz, tells of the river

> Deepening his voice with deepening of the night.

It is in this mystical hour that you will hear the most celestial and entrancing of all bird-notes, the songs of the thrushes,—the hermit, and the wood-thrush, and the veery. Sometimes, but not often, you will see the singers. I remember once, at the close of a beautiful day's fishing on the Swiftwater, I came out just after sunset into a little open space in an elbow of the stream. It was still early spring, and the leaves were tiny. On the top of a small sumac, not thirty feet away from me, sat a veery. I could see the pointed spots upon his breast, the swelling of his white throat, and the sparkle of his eyes, as he poured his whole heart into a long liquid chant, the clear notes rising and falling, echoing and interlacing in endless curves of sound,

> Orb within orb, intricate, wonderful.

Other bird-songs can be translated into words, but not this. There is no interpretation. It is music,—as Sidney Lanier defines it,—

> Love in search of a word.

But it is not only to the real life of birds and flowers that the little rivers introduce you. They lead you often into familiarity with human nature in undress, rejoicing in the liberty of old clothes, or of none at all. People do not mince along the banks of streams in patent-leather shoes or crepitating silks. Corduroy and homespun and flannel are the stuffs that suit this region; and the frequenters of these paths go their natural gaits, in calf-skin or rubber boots, or bare-footed. The girdle of conventionality is laid aside, and the skirts rise with the spirits.

A stream that flows through a country of upland farms will show you many a pretty bit of *genre* painting. Here is the laundry-pool at the foot of the kitchen garden, and the tubs are set upon a few planks close to the water, and the farmer's daughters, with bare arms and gowns tucked up, are wringing out the clothes. Do you remember what happened to Ralph Peden in *The Lilac Sunbonnet* when he came on a scene like this? He tumbled at once into love with Winsome Charteris,—and far over his head.

And what a pleasant thing it is to see a little country lad riding one of the plough-horses to water, thumping his naked heels against the ribs of his stolid steed, and pulling hard on the halter as if it were the bridle of Bucephalus! Or perhaps it is a riotous company of boys that have come down to the old swimming-hole, and are now splashing and gambolling through the water like a drove of white seals very much sunburned. You had hoped to catch a goodly trout in that hole, but what of that? The sight of a harmless hour of mirth is better than a fish, any day.

Possibly you will overtake another fisherman on the stream. It may be one of those fabulous countrymen, with long cedar poles and bed-cord lines; who are commonly reported to catch such enormous strings of fish, but who rarely, so far as my observation goes, do anything more than fill their pockets with fingerlings. The trained angler, who uses the finest tackle, and drops his fly on the water as accurately as Henry James places a word in a story, is the man who takes the most and the largest fish in the long run. Perhaps the fisherman ahead of you is such an one,—a man whom you have known in town as a lawyer or a doctor, a merchant or a preacher, going about his business in the hideous respectability of a high silk hat and a long black coat. How good it is to see him now in the freedom of a flannel shirt and a broad-brimmed gray felt with flies stuck around the band.

In Professor John Wilson's *Essays Critical and Imaginative*, there is a brilliant description of a bishop fishing, which I am sure is neither imaginative nor critical. "Thus a bishop, sans wig and petticoat, in a hairy cap, black jacket, corduroy breeches and leathern leggins, creel on back and rod in hand, sallying from his palace, impatient to reach a famous salmon-cast ere the sun leave his cloud, . . . appears not only a pillar of his church, but of his kind, and in such a costume is manifestly on the high road to Canterbury and the Kingdom-Come." I have had the good luck to see quite a number of bishops, parochial and diocesan, in that style, and the vision has always dissolved my doubts in regard to the validity of their claim to the true apostolic succession.

Men's "little ways" are usually more interesting, and often more instructive than their grand manners. When they are off guard, they frequently show to better advantage than when they are on parade. I get more pleasure out of Boswell's *Johnson* than I do out of *Rasselas* or *The Rambler*. The *Little Flowers of St. Francis* appear to me far more precious than the most learned German and French analyses of his character. There is a passage in Jonathan Edwards' *Personal Narrative,* about a certain walk that he took in the fields near his father's house, and the blossoming of the flowers in the spring, which I would not exchange for the whole of his dissertation *On the Freedom of the Will.* And the very best thing of Charles Darwin's that I know is a bit from a letter to his wife: "At last I fell asleep," says he, "on the grass, and awoke with a chorus of birds singing around me, and squirrels running up the tree, and some woodpeckers laughing; and it was as pleasant and rural a scene as ever I saw; and I did not care one penny how any of the birds or beasts had been formed."

Little rivers have small responsibilities. They are not expected to bear huge navies on their breast or supply a hundred-thousand horse-power to the factories of a monstrous town. Neither do you come to them hoping to draw out Leviathan with a hook. It is enough if they run a harmless, amiable course, and keep the groves and fields green and fresh along their banks, and offer a happy alternation of nimble rapids and quiet pools,

> With here and there a lusty trout,
> And here and there a grayling.

When you set out to explore one of these minor streams in your canoe, you have no intention of epoch-making discoveries, or thrilling and world-famous adventures. You float placidly down the long stillwaters, and make your way patiently through the tangle of fallen trees that block the stream, and run the smaller falls, and carry your boat around the larger ones, with no loftier ambition than to reach a good campground before dark and to pass the intervening hours pleasantly, "without offence to God or man." It is an agreeable and advantageous frame of mind for one who has done his fair share of work in the world, and is not inclined to grumble at his wages. There are few moods in which we are more susceptible of gentle instruction; and I suspect there are many tempers and attitudes, often called virtuous, in which the human spirit appears less tolerable in the sight of Heaven.

It is not required of every man and woman to be, or to do, something great; most of us must content ourselves with taking small parts in the chorus, as far as possible without discord. Shall we have no little lyrics because Homer and Dante have written epics? And because we have heard the great organ at Freiburg, shall the sound of Kathi's zither in the alpine hut please us no more? Even those who have greatness thrust upon them will do well to lay the burden down now and then, and congratulate themselves that they are not altogether answerable for the conduct of the universe, or at least not all the time. "I reckon," said a cow-boy to me one day, as we were riding through the Bad Lands of Dakota, "there's some one bigger than me, running this outfit. He can 'tend to it well enough, while I smoke my pipe after the round-up."

There is such a thing as taking ourselves and the world too seriously, or at any rate too anxiously. Half of the secular unrest and dismal, profane sadness of modern society comes from the vain idea that every man is bound to be a critic of life, and to let no day pass without finding some fault with the general order of things, or projecting some plan for its improvement. And the other half comes from the greedy notion that a man's life does consist, after all, in the abundance of the things that he possesseth, and that it is somehow or other more respectable and pious to be always at work making a larger living, than it is to lie on your back in the green pastures and beside the still waters, and thank God that you are alive.

Come, then, my gentle reader, (for by this time you see that this chapter is only a preface in disguise,—a declaration of principles or the want of them, an apology or a defence, as you choose to take it,) and if we are agreed, let us walk together; but if not, let us part here without ill-will.

You shall not be deceived in this book. It is nothing but a handful of rustic variations on the old tune of "Rest and be thankful," a record of unconventional travel, a pilgrim's scrip with a few bits of blue-sky philosophy in it. There is, so far as I know, very little useful information and absolutely no criticism of the universe to be found in this volume. So if you are what Izaak Walton calls "a severe, sour-complexioned man," you would better carry it back to the bookseller, and get your money again, if he will give it to you, and go your way rejoicing after your own melancholy fashion.

But if you care for plain pleasures, and informal company, and friendly observations on men and things, (and a few true fish-stories,) then perhaps you may find something here not unworthy your perusal. And so I wish that your winter fire may burn clear and bright while you read these pages; and that the summer days may be fair, and the fish may rise merrily to your fly, whenever you follow one of these little rivers.